The Other Side of Jordan

The Other Side of Jordan

By
Dawn Miller

INTEGRITY®
PUBLISHERS
Nashville

Scripture quotations used in this book are from the King James Version of the Bible (KJV).

Published in association with Alive Communications, 7680 Goddard Street, Suite 200, Colorado Springs, Colorado 80920.

Cover Design: David Uttley
            UDG | DesignWorks
            www.udgdesignworks.com

Interior Design: Inside Out Design & Typesetting

Library of Congress Cataloging-in-Publication Data

Miller, Dawn.
    The other side of Jordan / by Dawn Miller.
        p. cm.
    ISBN 1-59145-002-0 (pbk.)
        1. Women pioneers—Fiction.   2. Ranch life—Fiction. 3. Montana—Fiction.   I. Title.

PS3563.I376715O87 2003
813'.54–dc21

                                                2003003944

Printed in Canada
03 04 05 06 07 TCP 9 8 7 6 5 4 3 2 1

This book is dedicated to my son, Mitch . . . I can think of a lot of words, but there aren't enough to describe how much I love you.

PART ONE

On the Other Side
of Jordan

Here's your new journal Mama!

I asked Pa which part of the jorney we are on now, he said the Other side of Jordan. But Preacher says we still got to Pozess the Land. He says peoples toes curl when they think of facing The Enemy so they quit. I asked Preacher if Joshua's toes curled and he said no. He said God told Joshua not to be scared. I said if God told me not to be scared I'd go ahead and wade through that ol river and climb on up to the other side and not quit til I got my land.

I'd even go barefoot.

Your daughter,

Rose

P.S. Pa said for me to write on the next page too. He said it's a tre-dition.

So God told Joshua and the people to
GO FORTH and get what's yours. Be of
GOOD COURAGE, God said,
I got you this far, didn't I?

By Rose McGregor
13 years old
Montana Territory, 1873

October 17, 1873 . . .

*A*re you out there tonight, God? Because I could sure use some of your advice right along now. I know my mama always said if we looked hard enough, we would see you working even in the worst of people, but I admit I'm having a hard time of it.

Sometimes I feel like we've all lived ten lifetimes since we came to Montana four years ago, and sometimes, like today, I feel like we've come no further than that first shaky step we took out of our wagons—like we're still that ragtag group of drifters, still wandering, still looking for that place where we belong . . . especially after what happened in town today.

Quinn, of course, says I'm taking it too much to heart—that we all should remember who we are, not who someone *says* we are. He has always been that way with me, a great oak who's always there, always strong, always sturdy enough to stand against the battering winds that blow into our lives. But for all his sturdiness, my husband doesn't always understand everything about a woman's heart. And he wasn't in the mercantile when Leah Audrey said all she did, either.

We had all been so eager to take the trip to town, hoping for a little relief after the summer we've had . . . If the grasshoppers wasn't enough, those awful, greedy fires that swept through our valley over and over again through the summer had scorched more than just our grass but our spirits, too, and the proof of it was on every face as we climbed down from our wagons onto Audrey's hard, dusty main street. *Battle-weary* comes to mind . . . like soldiers searching for anything familiar to hold on to so they can leave behind the trying world they're in, even if it's only for a moment.

Even our little ones looked to be searching for something familiar as I watched them climb out, one by one: first John-Charles, then Patrick—but especially Rose, who hitched our baby, Mara Lee, on her hip, took Mercy by the hand, and made a quick beeline for the mercantile with a determined look on her face as she set off in search of the Audrey twins.

Once we were inside, me, Jessie, and Lillie got so busy gathering up news about the new church everyone was pitching in to build for Preacher, and dreaming over the bolts of goods we might get to buy one day, that I think we forgot our troubles for a moment. I say a moment because it wasn't long before we noticed Mrs. Pumphrey and Mrs. Spence—or Widow Spence, I should say—standing before us with excited looks on their faces.

Mrs. Pumphrey took a deep breath, her plump face set with determination, then went on to tell us that the ladies of Audrey had got together and decided it was high time a group was formed to get us all together once a month. "I figured we'd just call on each other like we've always done, but Mrs. Audrey says now that town's starting to take shape, we ought to do it up the *proper* way," she added, a slightly amused look in her eyes as she passed me the sheet of paper she held in her hand. "Sign here if you're up to it." Widow Spence smiled shyly like she always did, her salt-and-pepper bun bobbing at the back of her neck as we took turns signing our names to the paper. And it was right after Lillie had signed and turned to hand the paper to

Jessie that Mrs. Audrey appeared, and for reasons I still don't understand, she was bent on being nasty.

"Ah see you have the *whole* brood heah today," she said to me. Her dislike for our *brood* has gone from bad to worse since word of Jessie and her family trying to buy land for their "town of color" has spread throughout the territory. Jessie finished signing anyway, a look of grim satisfaction on her old brown face as she noticed Mrs. Audrey's surprise that she could write.

"Yes, we do tend to travel in *packs*," I said, feeling my cheeks burn as I watched Mrs. Audrey take the paper from Jessie's dark, leathery hand by pinching its edge between two fingers like it was dirty. She made what might pass for a smile, then turned abruptly toward Lillie like a cat about to pounce on a bird.

"Oh, and Miz Wade," she drawled, brushing back an invisible strand of blonde hair, "Ah believe ah met an old friend of yoahs the other day. She said she knew you in Virginia City. Lillie Lee—that was your *maiden* name, wasn't it?"

Lillie squared her small shoulders, said it was, then got straight to the point, asking Mrs. Audrey if the woman happened to work in the same gambling den as she had. Inside I cheered my sister-in-law's gumption, but I saw that it had cost her, too. Saw her smile had gone and bright pink spots had appeared on her cheeks.

"Ah'm not sure . . . but she did say you were so much more than just a dealer, dear," Mrs. Audrey drawled again, her dark eyes going mean. "*And* she seemed to think you were quite a shot with a gun, too. Said there was even a newspaper account of it."

I saw a sudden look of alarm cross Lillie's face as she glanced around for her stepson, John-Charles, my brother's quiet little half-Indian boy. But John-Charles was out front with my Patrick, helping the men load the supplies we'd be taking home. Rose and Mercy looked up only a moment, then turned back to their chatter with the Audrey twins.

"It's been said that a rumor without a leg to stand on will get around some other way, too—especially in this town," came Willa Cain's voice from behind us, and we all turned to see her standing there, looking like a pretty picture right out of *Harper's Weekly*—except for the way she had her arms folded across her chest and frowned at Mrs. Audrey. Mrs. Pumphrey looked amused again, and Widow Spence, shocked—although I don't know why. Even being engaged to Preacher hadn't softened Willa's sharp tongue when it came to dealing with gossips.

"It's all right, Willa," Lillie said, straightening herself up as she headed for the door, the rest of us not far behind her. "It's all right . . .

"Of all the times for trouble," I said once we were outside, feeling the lowness of it all creep over me. "But I guess that's when trouble does its best work."

"Ten minutes in that place, and *I* start feeling sorry for myself," Willa said with a sniff as she shut the door of the mercantile.

"Uh-huh," Jessie said, folding her arms across her chest like she always did when she was aggravated. I saw Mrs. Audrey had gotten to her, too.

"I know it sounds crazy," Lillie said as we stood together and watched the men finish their loading. "But all those years of living like I did in Virginia City, of seeing real ladies pass me by on the street without so much as a nod my way . . . well, I always promised myself one day I'd be one of them fine ladies, maybe even the head of some ladies club or such."

She stood there looking across the town, and there was such a little-girl wistful look on her face that I felt my heart want to reach out and hug the lonely young woman she had been. Lillie finally turned back around and gave us all a sheepish grin. "Don't matter how much I've tried to talk myself out of this foolishness. That girl is still inside me, and she won't give in."

"Well, maybe it's time she had her way," Willa said, a thoughtful look on her face. "I told Shawn just the other day that folks ought to stop trying to play God. Judging is his job, and I don't think he takes kindly to those who forget that."

"Well, it *is* my past," Lillie said with a frown. "No matter how far I've come, it seems to always find me."

"We all have pasts, Lillie," Willa said. "It's just that some have skeletons in their closets . . . and some have live bodies."

"I think I prefer skeletons. Skeletons can't *talk*," Lillie said with such childlike earnestness none of us could help smiling a bit at each other.

"Preacher says be of the world—not in it," Jessie said, speaking up. "An' that always sounded good to me, not to care what the world thinks. But I reckon sometimes it's hard not to care."

We all fell silent then, and I knew each of us in her own way was wishing the day had turned out different—or wishing that we *didn't* care. We watched Quinn and Jack lead one of our best heifers over to Mr. Audrey to pay for our meager supplies, then the men had the wagons ready and we were climbing in, waving our good-byes to Willa as she stood on the dusty boardwalk where the Audrey twins had joined her. The twins waved a reluctant good-bye to Rose, caught somewhere between their mama and pa's ways, as we started to roll past.

Rose finally turned from them, and I felt her watching me close for a bit, pursing her lips as she righted the bonnet that would be gone as soon as we were out of sight of town. But it was Patrick, who could sense my moods sometimes even before Quinn, who leaned forward from the back of the wagon, the baby cradled in his arms. "Mama," he said, soft-like, "will you look at Bird smile . . . "

I reached for my baby girl then, her toothless grin reminding me of Willa's words the day she was born: "I've never seen a baby come into the world so *merrily*," she'd said as we all wondered over such a smile on her face. A smile that had caused me to think so many times since then that she'd came to us knowing the end of some great story . . . and thought it might be fun to watch us all get there.

"*Mara Lee*," I corrected him like I always did, but Patrick had refused to call her anything but Bird since the day she'd peeked her little head of tousled curls over the rail of the crib at him and he'd said she looked just like a bird, waiting on supper.

"What an absolute bunch of outcasts," I heard Mrs. Audrey say as she joined her daughters outside the mercantile, watching our wagons roll out. I literally bit my tongue trying hard not to say anything. I glanced back down at Mara Lee, shiny black curls framing her little heart-shaped face as she stared up at me with those blue-gray eyes of hers. Then she laughed a huge belly laugh for such a little baby and grinned up at me again, and it was like she was saying, *The joke's on them, Mama—not us.*

I held on to that grin of hers the whole way home, through the bone weariness that settled in again from those long months of summer, from the disappointment of our trip gone bad and the hurt of Mrs. Audrey's hateful words . . .

But I felt the memory of Mara Lee's smile slip away from me as we pulled into our valley and I saw again the scorched hillsides standing stark against the setting sun. I felt Quinn studying me, remaining by my side even after everyone else had piled out of the wagons.

"What is it you're thinking, lass?" he said, pulling me close to him as I held our sleeping baby in my arms.

"I was just thinking this is the first time I'm actually wishing for an early snow," I said, and he followed my gaze to the hillsides.

"'Twould be a better sight, to be sure," he said gently, as if he sensed my hurt mood. Then he cocked his dark head to one side and turned me to look at him, his pale blue eyes searching my face. "But the grass would still be gone, wouldn't it? And an early snow would only make it worse on the cattle. Covering something up doesn't make it go away. Sometimes it makes things worse."

Now, as I write this, I have to wonder if that's what I'm doing, Lord, trying to cover up my fears so no one can see. I'm wondering if my sad turn of thought is really about the grasshoppers, the fires, or Mrs. Audrey—or if these are just the final straws.

Lately, it seems I am plagued more and more by fears I can't shake. Like a nightmare that has come to stay, returning again and again, I get these odd feelings . . . and find myself looking around expectantly for a great hand to snatch what I love out of my reach. *Trust in the Lord,* my heart says, and I do. But I'm ashamed to admit there is that small part of me that hesitates after I hand all that I love over to him. In my mind I see my hand still in midair, ready to pluck everything back just in case . . .

Just in case? How you must shake your head over me and my ways, Lord. But if I can't be honest with you, who can I be honest with? Who better to help me be honest with myself? You are my mirror that never leaves my side, forcing me to take a look even when I don't want to.

And that, I think, just might be one of my greatest blessings of all—even if I might not admit it to anyone else . . .

Help me to see what I need to see, Lord. Help me to have the faith of a child again . . . to, like Rose says, climb to the other side and not quit until I get there . . .

And maybe even do it barefoot.

October 18, 1873 . . .

Willa came to call this afternoon like she always does, in a flurry of dust and purpose. With Preacher gone for another week and our old friends Coy and Bonny off scouting land with Jessie's kids, it was clear to me that Willa was looking for company—or maybe something to take her mind off her worries . . . which is something we understood all too well.

We were hurrying to finish the canning, saying like we did every year that fall in Montana means looking over

your shoulder for winter while you work as fast as you can
to beat its coming. But I think we were trying to keep our
minds busy, too, trying not to think of that bad visit in
town or anything else that seemed to lie just under our
small talk. Willa took one look at us from the door of the
cabin, rolled up the sleeves of her fine dress, and pitched
right in. Our talk, of course, ended up turning to town and
Mrs. Audrey.

"Well, you can suit yourself, Lillie, as far as joining that
group of Mrs. Audrey's," Willa sniffed. "But I think I'd
prefer to stay the topic of lively gossip myself."

"Speakin' of gossip, when *are* you gonna marry that fine
man of your'n?" Jessie asked.

Willa arched a brow, but Jessie didn't budge in wanting
her answer. Willa sighed finally, knowing like the rest of us
that with Jessie, she wouldn't be able to help herself from
giving in.

"I told him we would marry as soon as the church is finished," she said, avoiding our eyes as she looked out the
window and gazed toward the mountains in the distance. I
don't know why, but there was something in the way she
said "finished" that stilled my hands from what they were
doing as she went on. "He has someone who's going to take
over the mission field once the church is done, you know.
That way, he won't have to go away anymore." She turned
back to us then and smiled. I guess it was her smile that
made me remember the day she had shown me those pictures of her parents that she had always kept with her and
how she said she would talk to them when she was lonely.
"I talk, they listen," she'd said, but by the look in her eyes
she could've added, *And they don't ever leave my side.*

I think Lillie sensed what Willa was feeling, too, for she said, "Life can be shaky, can't it, Willa?"

"If you're waitin' on life to quit bein' so shaky, chil', you're in for a long wait," Jessie said to no one in particular. I felt her words go through every one of us then, for I had no doubt they were meant for us all. And when Jessie turned to look back at me, I saw in that sweet, dark face of hers a lifetime of big trials and little triumphs in its lines and wrinkles, and I also saw that she understood.

Because she is one of us, too.

Quinn told me tonight while we were lying next to each other that he and Jack were going to have to bring the cattle down from the mountain pasture soon, that they had already stripped off what little grass there was left up there. He said if the cattle stayed up there much longer they would starve to death. He said he hoped the wild hay they had managed to cut before the fires would last. Then he asked me how much food stores we had left, and when I told him, he eased closer to me. "The Lord will see us through this, lass," he whispered, and we both fell silent. "Everything is going to be fine," he added after a while, breaking the silence.

I felt him search the covers then until he finally came to my hand, and when he took it in his own huge hand, covered with calluses, I heard him sigh.

I feel like we are all searching in the dark like that right now, Lord, reaching out to find your hand again . . . holding our breath until we do.

Sabbath morning, and everyone is still asleep . . . All but me and little Mara Lee here, draped under the little cloth I usually use to hide her nursing when company is around. For some odd reason, she has grown fond of it and gets too restless to nurse if I forget to cover her face . . . My funny little Bird, I wonder what your life will be like. I wonder if you will get as much joy as you give. I pray so . . .

This is the scripture I was led to just now: "Many waters cannot quench love, neither can the floods drown it"— Song of Solomon 8:7.

As I read it again aloud, Mara Lee pulled the cloth off her face to grin up at me . . .

October 20, 1873 . . .

I had quite a scare today—enough that my hands are still shaking as I write this. I don't know exactly how the team got so spooked, but it seemed to happen along about the time I was heading back from the spring with the water barrels for our wash. Patrick and John-Charles had just finished helping load them and had turned to go fetch their horses so they could join Rose with the cattle when the mules spooked for no reason I can explain. One minute I was hawing them up the hill, and the next thing I knew, Sassy, our oldest and gentlest mule, decided to take off in a dead run, giving Worthy no choice but to join her. Quinn ran out from the stables, hollering and waving his arms, trying to get them away from the deep ravine they were headed for, then Jasper and Honey joined in barking, even trying to bite at the mules' legs, but it felt like nothing was going to stop them.

Everything I saw seemed to me to slow down then. I remember feeling my bonnet fly off, felt the wind pulling the pins from my hair as I was jounced and jolted all over the front seat of that wagon. I remember seeing the shocked faces of the ones watching me as I flew past them, holding on to those reins for dear life, their helpless looks reminding me so much of the day we watched those flames roar through the valley.

It was Quinn who finally got close enough to dive onto the mules, yanking at Sassy's bridle as hard as he could while they dragged him along for a bit. Quinn finally jerked so hard on them that they swerved, then they stopped so quick the wagon tipped sideways and I was dumped to the ground.

Quinn picked me up and hugged me tight to him, and I know he must've felt something in me was ready to break because he kept holding me, saying, "Easy there, lass. All's well that ends well."

But when does it end? went through my mind to ask, but I didn't. Instead I let him lead me back toward the cabins, and when I saw how terrified the children were, I tried my best to smile.

"I didn't know ol' Sassy still had it in her," I said, trying to force cheer into my shaky voice. "Just goes to show you what an old lady can do when she sets her mind to it." I forced a chuckle then that I didn't exactly feel, and I heard Mara Lee chime in, laughter bubbling up out of the home-made baby buggy her little cousin Mercy had been pushing her around in.

"Oh, Mama," Rose choked out, her face streaked with tears. Patrick looked like he might get sick any minute, and John-Charles, like always, sat on his horse, the stoic little Indian, his mouth set in a thin line—but I'll never forget the tears I saw in his eyes.

"Well, it looks like Quinn here was the man for the job," Jack said, trying to joke away the bad of the moment. "He's always had a gift for dealing with stubborn ladies."

"Oh, hush," Lillie said, swiping at him with the dish-towel that was still in her hands as everyone crowded around me.

"Lord, chil', I think them guardian angels of your'n don't get a moment's rest," Jessie said then, hugging me. As she did, Lillie's eyes caught mine, and I saw by the look on her face she understood that life had went and gotten shaky on me again.

I waved them all away finally, saying I was fine. It wasn't until I shut the door of our cabin that I allowed myself a good cry. Then I cried for everything. I cried for our gardens that had been half ate up by grasshoppers, for our hay lands and the four years of work the fire had stole, I cried for the worry I'd seen in Quinn's eyes about how we were all going to survive the winter, even though he tried to hide it. I cried because it seems everything keeps going wrong no matter how hard we try . . .

But it was when I splashed some water on my face and took a quick glance in the mirror that I was so unnerved. For some reason the face that stared back looked almost like a stranger to me. Oh, my red hair was still there, and so was the spattering of freckles across my nose, but the glint of the fighter that I was used to seeing seemed to be gone.

How do I fight, Lord, when it seems like everything's been taken out of me? I thought then. *How do we possess this land like Preacher says when everything that's happened lately seems to tell us to leave?*

"Would to God that we had been content, and dwelt on the other side of the Jordan," Joshua had said when it seemed everything was going wrong, and I felt like I could've been the one who said those words myself. That's when Mercy's little voice startled me out of my thoughts.

"Aunt Callie, are you scared?" she said. I turned to see her standing in the door of my room, her golden curls so much like Lillie's, shining around her head like a little halo. Mara Lee, who is near half her size already, was perched comically on her hip, and I reached out and took her, trying to busy myself with her changing so I could think of how to answer. As if sensing my mood, Mercy watched me with a kind of patient understanding that always amazed me for one so young. If being born too soon had made her small, God had made up for it by the giant heart she had for others. It never ceased to amaze me how perceptive and well-spoken this child, not yet four, could be.

"Sometimes I get scared," I said finally, and Mercy nodded and walked around the bed, running her fingers over the stitching of my quilt.

"Mama says God doesn't give us fear," she said, then she came back over and sat down next to me, putting her little hand in my own as she looked up into my eyes with such a thoughtful look to her tiny face. "So, if he doesn't give it to us, that means we don't have to keep it, right, Aunt Callie?"

"No, we don't," I said, trying to blink back my tears. Mercy smiled, satisfied with my answer, and then she took her leave, a child again, skipping back outside to find Rose and the others.

To have the faith of a child again . . . my own words, my own prayer, has come back to me again today as I put this all to paper. I do pray, Lord, to feel that kind of faith again in me—the kind I saw shining in Mercy's eyes. There is such a simple beauty in that kind of trust. It's no wonder you say those are the kinds of hearts that will enter heaven. I know I couldn't think of better company myself . . .

I read another Bible story to the children tonight after dinner. I admit, I was so weary from all that happened I could barely keep my eyes open—but it is "tre-dition," as Rose likes to say, and I sensed their needing something familiar to hold on to, too, by the way they wordlessly gathered to me after dinner. Truth is, there was something comforting for me as well, having them sprawled all around me on the floor as I rocked Mara Lee to sleep. Patrick was the one to pick the story of Gideon and the angel, but after I finished it, it was clear he wasn't happy with Gideon.

"Well, Gideon must've been crazy," Patrick said, always right to the point. "If a real live *angel* showed up to me, I think that'd be enough proof. I wouldn't have to set out no ol' piece of sheepskin to see if it got wet."

"I think Gideon was just scared," I said, patting Patrick's arm. Then I looked over at Mercy. "But you know what? A real good friend of mine told me that God doesn't give us fear, so that means we don't have to keep it—and Gideon learned that, too."

"I bet that friend was Mercy," Rose said knowingly, brushing a hand over Mercy's curls. "I can tell because Mercy's cheeks are all red now."

"'Bout as red as your hair," John-Charles teased, and they all laughed—even Rose—and I noticed something new in their laughter: a strength I hadn't realized before. I wonder even now as I write this if their wanting to be read to was a way of moving on, too, past the bad of the day.

"I still say he should've knowed better," Patrick said, unwilling to give up his point, and it was along about that time I looked up to see Lillie standing in the room, watching us, and when our eyes met, she smiled a wry kind of smile that said, *We should all know better.* I watched her bundle up Mercy to send her on her way to their cabin with John-Charles, and I couldn't help thinking again how pretty Lillie was with her little turned-up nose like Mercy's and her golden-brown curls that always seem to escape her bun. Rose and Patrick climbed the ladder for their own beds not long after, and as Lillie and I sat talking quietly, I confessed to her I wondered if I hadn't been waiting on proof myself instead of just having faith.

"I had a room I kept above the saloon where I worked," she said then. "And every morning I used to stare out the window, watching people going up and down the street below." Lillie got up and added a piece of wood to the fire, talking with her back to me. "Everyone seemed to be going somewhere but me. Seemed like the whole world knew how to live their lives but me . . . But you know what I found out, Callie? I found out there ain't a one of us that really knows how—we're all just learning along the way

. . . I almost told Mrs. Audrey that, too. I almost said, 'You don't know where I've been, how I got there, and you don't know where I'm going, either.'" Lillie looked over her shoulder at me then and smiled a small kind of smile. "But something kept me from saying it. Maybe *Someone*. I think I know why, too; I think it's because Mrs. Audrey's learning, too."

I admit I felt humbled by Lillie's forgiving heart . . . by her goodness . . . but I felt grateful, too, to have her in my life, and I couldn't help going over and hugging her. "I hope I'm learning, too," I whispered then, feeling my eyes well up with tears. When she pulled back from me, I saw her eyes were shiny, too, and it hit me that it was the first time we'd been able to share such a moment since all the trouble.

"We're all learning," she said, taking a shaky breath as she smiled. "It's like Jessie says, 'You're not dead until you die, so you might as well live.'"

"Jessie *would* say that," I said, shaking my head, but before any more could be said, Quinn came in from checking on the cattle with Jack. He took one look at us then went to busying himself with carrying the water into the kitchen, whistling as he did it. Lillie smiled as she shrugged into her shawl—common knowledge was that Quinn's whistling was a sign he wasn't sure what to do next—and we walked to the door together. As I watched her make her way down to her own cabin, I thought of what she had said.

It seems at every turn lately, the Lord has been speaking to my heart. I said a quick prayer of thanks to him for that, and when I stepped back inside the cabin, I saw Quinn standing in the middle of the room with a surprise for me:

tiny yellow-hearted daisies he had found growing in a split of rock on the side of the mountain. The only place, he informed me, where the wind wasn't blowing and a bit of sun shone.

"Do you remember the first time I gave you flowers like that?" he said, smiling softly, and I nodded, trying to blink back the tears. Then I got the idea to fetch my first journal and find the entry that told of that first day he gave me flowers all those years ago on that wagon train headed west. We sat like kids, cross-legged, in front of the fireplace as I turned the pages of that old journal, finally coming to the entry I was looking for. I was surprised to find the daisy he'd given me that day still tucked safely in the crease of the page. I held it up, letting the firelight dance off its dried petals, and saw Quinn's wind-burned face go soft with memories.

"Do you remember what I said to you that day?" he asked softly as he reached forward to touch my hair.

"Well, yes, it's right here," I said, looking down at the pages so as not to cry.

"But do you remember, lass?" he prodded again, and I felt a single tear slip down my cheek as he hugged me to him.

"Yes, I remember," I whispered finally. "You said they were tiny but tough—just like me."

"I didn't remind you to make you cry," Quinn said, and I heard the emotion in his deep voice. Then he pulled back from me, and when he looked down into my eyes I felt like we were back on that trail again, just him and me under a dark, dark sky that went on forever. "I reminded you because I thought you might have forgot."

I'm pressing this new flower in this page . . . so I don't forget.

October 21, 1873 . . .

I guess my crying the other day didn't go as unnoticed as I thought. If there hasn't been enough excitement around here lately, it seems the children had to try and make some more, but if nothing else, it's made us all laugh again. Now that it's over, that is . . .

It all started when I accidentally overheard Rose, Patrick, and John-Charles talking. I was coming back from Lillie's with a thimble of hers I'd borrowed to do some mending when I caught a movement out of the corner of my eye just behind the corrals and saw just a peek of a dark head of hair as Patrick took off his hat.

"Mama was *crying*, I'm telling you," Patrick was saying. "Mercy told John-Charles last night, and he told me. Didn't you, John-Charles?"

I saw another shadowy figure, hands shoved in his pockets, and heard John-Charles clear his throat. "Yes, but I wasn't supposed to tell it. She just said pray because Mama and Jessie looked sad and Aunt Callie looked like she'd been crying. Mercy's always sayin' things like that."

"Yeah, but *she* never lies," Rose said knowingly, and I saw her skinny elbow come out to rest on the fence railing. "I think it's that ol' Mrs. Audrey's doing. I *still* say there's something about her. I read that desperadoes on the run sometimes go into hiding and pretend to be someone else so's they don't get caught." She took a breath then said, "But livin' the lie catches up with 'em 'cause all the meanness don't have nowhere to go, and it just comes bustin' out all of a sudden."

"Aw, Rose, she's just spiteful, is all," Patrick said, impatient after three years of suffering through Rose's insistence that Mrs. Audrey was the "Banditti of the Plains" she'd read about in those awful dime novels. But then with a bit more gruffness than I've ever heard in his voice, he added, "But she *does* need to be taught a lesson."

"Pa says women need us to look out for them," John-Charles added with a note of duty. "And Mama, Aunt Callie, and Jessie are about the best ones I know of."

"Well, don't you even think of leaving me out of what you're planning," Rose said, insisting on being a part of what she thought might be a great adventure. "I might be a girl," she said, "but I can ride better and faster than either of you."

It didn't take long after that for me to hear that they figured riding into town at night and scaring the daylights out of Mrs. Audrey was a pretty good start—nor did it take long for me to find Quinn and Jack down at the barn and tell them of our children's plot. But instead of confronting them like I thought they would, the two men decided it would be "first rate" to follow them out and wait until they got good and lost.

"That's about the best time to close in on 'em, too," Jack said, "when they're scared half out of their heads." He grinned at me, and Quinn matched the grin with one of his own. When I told them it was no wonder our children acted the way they did, they grinned again . . .

We are now waiting for the prisoners to be brought in, Jessie, Lillie, and me. Mercy is wheeling a dozing Mara Lee around in the carriage, looking almost half-asleep herself.

"Sakes alive, Callie, put that pen down," Jessie says as I write this. "I'm on pins and needles 'bout them little ones, an' that scratchin' sound don't help."

I'll say this, then end it: I think our Jessie is on "pins and needles" more about Rose than anything . . . that her "little sis" could do such a thing is more than Jessie can imagine. I just looked up to see Lillie smiling at me like she knows what I'm thinking. Most likely, she does.

More later . . .

Our wayward group has returned, and never was there a more forlorn-looking bunch than Rose, Patrick, and John-Charles as they shuffled into the cabin with Quinn and Jack behind them. Rose looked like she had been through a war, her long, honey-red hair all askew. Patrick and John-Charles just looked white from fear.

It was then that Mercy woke up from the settee and spotted them.

"Rose!" Mercy yelled, running to her like a little mother to help her up the stairs to the loft.

"I think I can make it," Rose whispered dramatically, not daring to look at me or Lillie—but especially avoiding Jessie, who had crossed her arms the minute the door opened and was tapping her foot against the floor.

It wasn't until we got Patrick and John-Charles off to bed as well that we got the full story of what happened.

Quinn and Jack waited until the kids were almost out of the valley before they stepped up their pace, following just a short distance behind the little group. And that's when it seemed Rose (the fearless leader) started to lose her sense of direction. First she led them off to the left then edged a bit to the right and finally, realizing she was lost, resorted to making a deal with God.

"Put your hands together," Rose had suddenly announced, holding a hand up to stop the procession, then she put her own hands together and began to pray: "God, if you help us find our way out of here, I promise I'll be good," she said, then hesitated for a moment. "But let's make me bein' good start tomorrow because if we *can* find town, I'm going to tell that ol' Mrs. Audrey what we think of her hurtin' Mama's and Jessie's and Aunt Lillie's feelin's—*after* we scare her real good."

"I think we should say amen real loud, Rose," Patrick added. "Just to make sure he hears."

"Well, what if he doesn't agree with the deal?" John-Charles said, and Patrick let out a loud sigh.

"Amen *seals* the deal, don't it, Rose?"

"Near as I can tell," Rose said. "So let's do it."

They all hollered, "Amen!" and that's when Quinn and Jack came galloping in, scaring the life out of them all. Quinn said Rose's first words after she caught her breath were, "Don't scalp me! My cousin's an Indian."

I don't think any of us laughed so hard in our lives. Even after Quinn and I turned in for the night, we'd fall silent then start laughing again. Then the silences got longer, and I thought he had finally fallen off to sleep when I felt him turn to his side suddenly and peer at me in the dark.

"Lord, I promise to be a good husband to Callie," Quinn whispered gravely. "But I promise to be good startin' *tomorrow* because tonight—" He turned and started to tickle my sides unmercifully, and as I began to laugh, so did he. We laughed and laughed like kids in spite of everything that had happened, and as we did, I realized again how much I loved the sound of our laughter together—and how much I had missed hearing it lately.

When I got up to check on Mara Lee, hearing Quinn's and my laughter still echoing in my ears, I couldn't help but come and write this. To remember. Even an echo of laughter can make you smile like you hadn't smiled in a very long time.

October 23, 1873 . . .

Cloudy and cold this morning. There's a mist coming off the mountains that stretches down across the valley like long fingers. Jasper and Honey bark, snapping at the mist, then they run back to where Quinn, Jack, and the boys are saddling up. Patrick and John-Charles look tuckered out from the work load their pa's have heaped on them, but neither of them has complained. Paying penance has made it a very quiet two days—but busy just the same. Rose and I have just finished churning five pounds of butter and are making ginger cakes for Jessie and Lillie's visit. We've decided to spend the afternoon together sewing. Rose, who usually would rather be hung over a cliff with a mess of snakes crawling over her (Rose's own words) than sew, is handling her dilemma bravely. She's even managed to smile a weak smile at me a few times as she stirs the batter . . .

I suppose I spoke too soon on Rose. We were maybe a half-hour into our sewing when I saw her mask start to crumble—even in spite of Mercy's efforts to cheer her.

Rose, looking like she couldn't bear it anymore, sighed and set her sampler on her lap, looking from me to Lillie and finally even to Jessie. "Well, doesn't it say *anywhere* in the Bible that we're supposed to protect our family?"

"Protecting your family isn't plotting to scare someone half to death, Rose," I said, trying to keep a straight face as Lillie glanced my way with a twinkle in her eye.

"'Vengeance is mine; I will repay, saith the Lord,' it says right here," Jessie said, tapping her gnarled old finger against a page in the Bible.

"Yes ma'am," Rose said, trying to blink back the tears of a prodigal daughter. We watched her jab at her sampler with the needle, and when she looked up again it was as if a thought had suddenly occurred to her.

"I'm sure glad I taught you how to read, Jessie," she added, then bent her head back down over her sewing. Jessie, Lillie, and I couldn't help but smile, for everything in her voice said at that moment she wasn't very glad at all.

October 25, 1873 . . .

I spent the better part of this evening filling and refilling and heating water for the washtub so we could all be ready to leave early for church in the morning. I was so looking forward to hearing Preacher speak again that I didn't mind the work—neither did Quinn—even as tired as we both were. Rose and Patrick, on the other hand, acted like prisoners facing the gallows come morning. Even after we had sent them off for bed, faces scrubbed and prayers said, Quinn and I could hear them whispering worriedly amongst themselves up in the loft. Then we watched as Patrick climbed back down first, Rose following reluctantly.

"Mama, do you think God told Preacher what we did?" he said, looking from me to Quinn like he wasn't sure he wanted to hear our answer.

"I think if God wants Preacher to know, he'll tell him," Quinn answered somberly, and Rose and Patrick looked at each other with dread. Mara Lee slapped her hands in the water, then laughed when it splashed against her face, looking at all of us as if to ask if we had seen her new trick.

"Well, at least Bird's happy," Patrick said with resignation.

"Sure, *she* can be happy," Rose said with a large sigh of resignation herself. "She's a baby—she ain't done nothin' yet."

October 26, 1873 ...

Sabbath. Jessie is forever saying she thinks God whispers straight into Preacher's ear, the way he knows just how to plant the right seeds in our hearts to grow, and I have to admit, today seemed to be proof of that. Such a full day. I will try to record everything as it happened ...

Before dawn even broke, we were hurrying to get on our Sunday best. We had mended our clothes over so much that I worried they wouldn't survive another wash, but thankfully, they did. Mercy and Mara Lee looked like

little china dolls in the matching dresses and bonnets
Lillie and I had cut down from one of Rose's old calicoes.
Rose looked pretty as a picture as well, but her eyes were
solemn. Patrick and John-Charles were somber little
affairs, too, with their slicked-back hair and too-tight
shoes. Every one of us needs new shoes—my own being
stuffed with so much paper at the toes to make up for the
hole in the soles that Quinn teased me that I "crinkled"
when I walked. Or tried to tease, I should say, for I saw the
hurt of it in his eyes when he said it, and I put my hand on
his arm and patted it.

"At least you'll be able to tell where I'm at," I said,
trying to get him to smile. He cocked his handsome head
sideways, looking at me before he pulled his hat down.

"'Tis a comfort knowin' you canna sneak up on me," he
said, smiling a small smile as he hawed the team on.

I don't recall much about the trip, other than we were
fairly warm in spite of the chill—that, and I wondered
what Mrs. Audrey thought of her proper town with two
huge bull elk standing in the middle of the road, pawing
and snorting and refusing to let folks get by. But we did get
by finally and made our way, quick, inside Preacher's tent
to get a good seat, along with everyone else in the territory. Mrs. Pumphrey and Widow Spence were already
seated alongside Mr. and Mrs. Audrey, the twins next to
them. I saw Rose glance over toward them briefly, then she
spotted Preacher coming from the back and motioned for
Patrick and John-Charles to hurry and sit before he saw
them. Mercy hurried, too, though she didn't really understand why.

Preacher walked to the front of the tent with his Bible

in one hand, touching shoulders and saying his hellos, then turned to face us with a smile once he got to the front. Willa sat in the second row of chairs with us, looking up at him like he hung the moon, and judging by the feelings of the rest of the crowd, you might wonder if he did. Preacher started right in, like he always did, his deep voice strong and gentle, causing you to feel his words. And we did . . . every one of us did. Lord, help me remember exactly what he said . . .

"I've been wondering about some things I'd like to share with you all, if you don't mind," Preacher began, looking around the tent.

A few people called out, "Go on, Preacher," and he smiled again.

"I know most of you well enough by now to know you thought coming to this territory was like finding your Promised Land. I know, too, that these last months have left a lot of doubts in your minds about that thought. But what I want you to ask yourselves now is whether you've really crossed over to that other side of Jordan to the Promised Land yet. *Have* you left your old lives behind— left behind any old fears or old ways of looking at things? Or are you still standing on the banks, afraid to move forward, afraid to take hold of what God has promised you? Sometimes I wonder . . ."

He looked around the crowded tent. "Now, don't get me wrong," he said. "I know everyone's been through some real tough times this past year. But the truth is, I don't think God puts us through as much adversity as we like to think. I think we put ourselves through more by not letting go. Tell you what else: I think he just waits for us to get so sick of wallowing in our trouble we're finally willing to take the risk—the risk that his plan might just be *better* than ours . . .

"The children of the Israelites were born risktakers. They had cut their teeth in the wilderness, and they knew with every fiber of their beings that God had something better for them. They didn't look back because they already knew what was there. Instead, they followed God toward their future . . . and when they snuck into Jericho, they found another risktaker.

"Her name was Rahab."

Preacher kind of leaned his elbows on the pulpit then, like he was getting ready to share something good. "Now, the funny thing is," he said slowly, "most people would think the children of God might have a problem striking a bargain with a known prostitute . . . "

I glanced over quick at Lillie and saw her eyes go wide as Preacher went on.

"But you see, her title meant no more to them than their old address. All they saw was another child who had been a slave to the wilderness—another child who had the faith to believe God would set her free, too. The good Lord honors faith like that, too.

"I know most folks don't like reading down that line of 'begats' in the first chapter of Matthew, but if you did, you just might find that some impressive descendants came from Rahab the prostitute . . . " Preacher ducked his head and looked at his Bible. "Let's see: It says Salmon begat Boaz by *Rahab* . . . Then Boaz begat Obed by Ruth, and Obed begat Jesse, and Jesse—why, he begat David the king." Preacher smiled with satisfaction then ducked his head again, looking back to where he'd marked his place.

He ran his finger down a ways then rapped the Book with his finger. "Now, here's a name that comes a little farther down that same line—I think you might just recognize it."

Preacher looked back up at us, his eyes passing over every single one of us in the tent.

"His name is Jesus. '*Jesus*, a descendant of Rahab the prostitute?' you ask. He was . . . and, my friends, he was one of the greatest risktakers of all times. He risked everything on a world that had fallen so far down its people forgot that all they had to do was look up and reach out their hands to God.

"Jesus knew God is almighty. In the Gospel of Luke, it was Jesus himself who said he had stood and watched Satan fall like lightning from heaven. And yet Jesus 'made himself of no reputation' . . . and came 'in the likeness of men: And . . . as a man, he humbled himself, and became obedient unto death, even the death of the cross.'

"Have any of you ever really thought about Jesus' death? Have you thought about what filled his mind as he faced the cross? Well, I think He was *afraid*."

Preacher paused then, looking around the room again, and for just a moment I could've swore his eyes met mine. Then he went on talking.

"Think about it: The Son of Man, knowing what's to come, is all alone, kneeling in the garden to pour out his fears to our Father. Scripture says he was sorrowful and deeply distressed, but that in agony he *prayed more earnestly*. And his prayer was, 'Not my will, but thine, be done.'

"Jesus looked past his fears and took that risk because he knew who God was, who God *is* . . . "

As Preacher fell silent, I glanced around the tent and saw that Mrs. Audrey's cheeks were bright red—but so were mine, judging by the hot feel of them, because Preacher had spoken to my heart as well. He'd touched all our hearts. I saw Lillie looking like she'd just been told the best news she'd ever heard. Jessie was nodding with big tears in her eyes, and Willa looked more amazed than I ever saw.

"Until we can understand that the same God who made this earth is the same God we pray to," Preacher went on, "that he's the same God who promises us victory if we only believe . . . until then, none of us will cross over to the other side of Jordan. And know this: There are some who may even drown in the crossing." Preacher looked around with a sad look to his eyes then finished his sermon.

"My prayer for you is that you *don't* drown. But instead, you lift your hands up out of that water and let God pull you out. Take the risk, folks. Take the risk!"

We waited, silent in our own thoughts about what he'd said, until Preacher had walked past us down the aisle, then we began to file out. I felt Quinn take my hand, and when I looked up at him, he smiled. Then I saw Lillie fairly pull Jack with her to join us in the line shuffling out.

Jack was the first to speak. He cleared his throat and reached out and shook Preacher's hand. "That was a fine talk, Preacher," he said. "Ain't every day an ol' risktaker from the wrong side gets to hear what it would be like to take a risk for something right."

"I felt the same way some years back," Preacher chuckled, and that's when Lillie stepped up, looking from Preacher to Willa with tears in her eyes.

"Did you say anything?" Lillie asked, and Willa beamed, shaking her head.

"Didn't have time," she said. "I suppose that makes it even better, doesn't it?"

"It didn't even matter," Lillie said softly, shaking her head in amazement. "God didn't even care what Rahab was. He just saw her faith . . . and he remembered her for it . . . "

"Well, I seem to recall a little girl sayin' once that Jesus ain't no *suspector* of persons," Jessie said from somewhere behind us, and we all laughed. I saw Rose cringe then as the attention was turned to her, and she quickly grabbed ahold of Patrick and John-Charles, scampering out of the line before Preacher could see them. Preacher shook his head, looking at us all like he wasn't sure what he had missed, then he caught sight of Mercy and smiled.

"Well, Mercy Wade," Preacher said, bending down to shake her tiny hand. When his large hand covered her own, Mercy's eyes went wide as if she was seeing her hand disappear for good. "So this is what a miracle looks like in a bonnet and dress . . . " We all smiled, and Mercy smiled proudly along with us. She knew the story of her birth now as well as the rest of us.

I didn't say a word about the fear part of Preacher's sermon—but I don't think I had to, the thoughtful way Preacher caught my eye as he looked up from Mercy.

We had to move on then to allow Preacher and Willa to tell the rest of the congregation their good-byes, and that's when I saw Mr. and Mrs. Audrey standing behind us. Mrs. Audrey gave us a long kind of considering look, like she was trying to find how she really felt, then she shook her head and turned away. I could've sworn I saw Mr. Audrey look at her, sad, like he understood more of what was going on than she thought.

We headed for the wagons not long afterward, and that's

when we saw Peach in his usual spot, waiting on us. Peach, like everyone else who'd stumbled into our lives—and maybe even for reasons I still haven't figured—had decided he liked us well enough to come calling when he saw fit. And Sunday was one of those days. He never set foot inside the church. Instead he waited for us outside the tent, sitting in his old wagon, whittling on a piece of wood.

Today, though, he had company. At first I thought the boy to be about sixteen, seventeen years old, but when he looked up, I saw it was just his size that had fooled me. His face was as young as Rose's, but now that I think on it . . . maybe old, too, like he had seen more than his fair share of life. He looked up at us briefly, his dark eyes taking in our whole group, then he slowly walked away, and it wasn't until we got to our picnic spot that I found out anything about him. And that was after we got over the shock of seeing Peach with his new teeth.

Jack was the first to notice, and as is Jack's way, he couldn't let it go without saying something.

"Why, Peach, you're looking real shiny with them new teeth," Jack teased. "Who you gettin' gussied up for?"

"Maybe it's Widow Spence," Lillie said, the dimples in her cheeks coming out as she grinned.

Peach looked at Lillie, startled, like she might have guessed his secret, then was quick to compose himself as he turned back to Jack. "And as far as gettin' gussied up, ain't nothin' doin'," he said, shaking his grizzled old head. "Last feller I heard of went all out with a full dippin', ended up gettin' his ears so plugged he never heard a drop of sound agin."

We all laughed then, and it wasn't until Jessie, Lillie,

and I had made plates for everyone that I thought of the boy again and asked Peach who he was.

"The Norton boy—can't tell ya much 'bout him," he said. "But what I kin say is, he's a real hard worker. Been up to my place to help me a time or two. Wouldn't give a plug nickel for his folks, though."

"Zora and Nora, they say he's next door to a perfect heathen," Rose offered, and Patrick grinned, tipping his hat back from his head in a way that reminded me so much of Quinn. Escaping the possibility of Preacher being disappointed in them had put them all in a better mood.

"Those ol' twins don't know nothin'," Patrick said, crossing his arms. "He lives on the old Posey ranch, Rose. Ain't nobody *next door* to him for miles."

"I don't know anything about him being a heathern," Peach said.

"What *is* a heathern, Peach?" Rose asked, taking on his slang like it was second nature, and Peach cleared his throat, trying not to smile.

"Well, Miss Rose, I'm figurin' you're lookin' at one."

"But I thought *heathen* meant you didn't believe in God," John-Charles said, studying Peach with new interest, and all the children's heads turned to stare at Peach then.

"Well, I reckon I don't," Peach said, avoiding their stares.

"Well, who do you talk to, then?" Rose pressed him, ignoring Quinn's and my looks.

"I talk to myself," Peach said, and Rose looked at him curiously.

"Well, I always have a lot to talk about," Rose said.

"But I think even I'd get pretty bored if it was just me doing all the talking *and* the listening. And lonely, too."

It was then that I saw Mercy quietly slip her little hand in Peach's, saw Peach's eyes crinkle at the corners with what might have passed as a smile as he looked down at her, and suddenly there was a different look on his face, kind of thoughtful, but something else, too.

Of all things, it was precocious little Mercy who broke the mood. She stared up into Peach's kind old face with such a wistful look that I thought she was going to say something real sweet, like she had done to me before. Instead she said, "Can you take them teeth out, Peach?"

What remained of our proper little picnic was over as our children jumped up and surrounded the dear old trapper, exclaiming with the kind of oohs and aahs usually reserved for a traveling circus as a fine set of snowy new teeth were extracted and shown about with all the flourish of a magician producing a rabbit out of thin air.

Thank you, Lord, for this day. For Preacher's words and for this wonderful, crazy bunch I call my family. I couldn't imagine my life without them.

October 27, 1873 . . .

It's a cold, windy day—a lot colder than yesterday, in fact, colder than it's been all month. Fall appears to be on its way out a lot quicker this year—which is why I decided to make a quick work of lunch so I could ride out with the men to start rounding up our cattle. Lillie got the same idea as me, but Jessie was having none of it.

"No ma'am," Jessie said, shivering as she eyed the men adjusting their saddles down by the barn. "The good Lord gave me feet to use, and I reckon I'll keep them on the ground today. You just leave me them babies, and we'll both be happy."

We knew Jessie had been lonely with her own family gone and Rose back in the saddle now that her punishment was over, so we obliged, bringing her an ecstatic Mercy and Mara Lee (who wasn't sure what Mercy's excitement was about, but was glad to join in), and off we went.

I don't think Lillie and me have ever been so cold in our lives—but so glad we went, too. As we moved away from the dull, burnt hills of the valley and began the steep climb to the mountain pastures, color sprang up everywhere, from the reds and oranges in the trees to the wide blue-gray sky that hung over us like a bowl to the dark black peaks of the mountains proudly sporting their first caps of snow. The horses got friskier as we climbed, too—especially Midnight, who is almost as comical as her mistress, Rose, when it comes to antics. She pawed the earth and rubbed her nose in it so often that she soon had what looked like a brown, shaggy beard on her face, causing us to laugh.

When we got to the mountain pasture, we didn't find as many of the cows as we expected, but the ones we found were work enough. Some tried to double back, and some went for the ravines while others dodged us, squeezing their bulky bodies through stands of lodgepole pine that defied the imagination. By the time we were to the halfway point of the mountain, I was getting good at feeling when they were going to try and make a break for it. Lillie was, too, and we grinned at each other from time to time when we'd bring a straggler back in. Rose, Patrick, and John-Charles were old hats at it, and I couldn't help marvel at their horsemanship, as young as they are, whipping around the herd, hawing them like old cowhands. I noticed something else, too. I noticed that without us even trying, we were all moving and working together, wordlessly, like we sensed each other's moves.

I think Preacher's sermon did us good, too, for we all seemed determined to keep our spirits up in spite of the worry over where the rest of the herd might be.

"You look just as pretty as the day we first met," Quinn said, sidling up next to me with his horse as he reached for a wayward strand of my hair. Jack picked that time to come trotting up.

"Yes, she's always been a looker," he said, grinning his slow, easy grin, "but them lookers are hard to handle—I should know."

"Should know what?" Lillie called out, and we all laughed. Lillie frowned prettily. "Never mind," she said. "Maybe I *don't* want to know." Which made us laugh harder.

Such a good day in spite of the work . . . I wish I could capture it to paper, what it was like watching us all walking together to the corrals once we made it in—Rose, Patrick, and John-Charles's tired laughter rising up to mingle with the churned-up dust tinted orange by the low afternoon sun . . . Jack draping his arm over Lillie's shoulder as they walked together . . . and Quinn, turning to look over his shoulder to see where I was . . .

Jack asked if I would go with him after dinner to watch John-Charles with the wild mustangs, and as tired as I was, I was still eager to go with him. It had been a long while since I'd taken a walk with my brother, and it brought back old memories of us as kids, walking the farm in Missouri together. We talked about those times as we walked, about how he had planned to be a rich and famous gambler and I had planned to travel the world and write my adventures as I went.

"We weren't too far off, Jack," I said as we walked. "You gambled, and I wrote journals—still do. God just changed our minds about what you gamble on and what I write about."

Jack grinned. "It's a good thing he did, too, sis," he said. "It's a good thing." And then we stopped just a short distance away from where John-Charles sat, patiently watching the herd. It never ceases to amaze me how the mustangs always find their way back to our ranch just before winter hits. This time, though, they were staying closer to the river, with the grass as poor as it is, munching on anything green left to find near the banks.

We watched John-Charles slip off his seat on the outcropping of rock and cross over the little gully as he headed for the river, armed with just a halter he would use to bring one in. He only brought in what we needed and no more, Jack said. What we saw next was like watching poetry.

John-Charles edged closer to the herd, and I could see by the way he headed for some of the horses to the right that he had an idea which one he was going to pick. The horses immediately sensed him, and I saw that one of them in particular kept its eyes right on John-Charles. Jack told me that would be the one. We watched as John-Charles took what he called the lead-mare stance, squaring his shoulders to the horse as he stared eye to eye with the horse. The mustang immediately cantered off a short distance, and John-Charles turned to him again, standing between it and the rest of the herd and silently telling the horse he was calling the shots and that it could rejoin the herd when John-Charles said. Finally the horse slowed its trot and dropped its nose to almost an inch above the ground. Then we saw John-Charles turn sideways, looking slightly away from the horse. Suddenly the horse stopped and turned to face John-Charles. Then it walked right up to John-Charles, its nose just inches away from my nephew's shoulder. John-Charles gently slipped the halter over the mustang's head and then turned around and began to slowly lead the horse toward us, smiling easily as he spotted us from the distance, like what he'd done was the most natural thing in the world.

Rose had learned some of the same moves after watching John-Charles one full summer and studying what he did. One day she led a horse right up to the cabin, haltered by the drawstring from her petticoat. The memory still makes me smile. Made Jack smile today, too, when I reminded him of it.

"I never did figure out how she managed to do that until I heard John-Charles explain it one day. Still, it doesn't seem real," I said, and Jack smiled, soft-like, then looked back out toward the river where John-Charles was still making his way toward us.

"He says they talk more with just a look than we do

with a whole lot of words," Jack said. "Sometimes I think he's so used to being around them he forgets how to talk around us." He turned and looked at me then and said, "I know it sounds crazy, but I was almost glad that he went with Rose and Patrick like that."

"Well, when you put it like that, I guess I'm glad, too," I said, and we both smiled at each other. "I'm glad you let him do as he saw fit with those mustangs, too," I added. Jack nodded.

"I did it for me as much as him, sis," he said, "to make him feel a part of this land."

I didn't say anything then, but I knew Jack meant a part of the family, too, with John-Charles being torn between his real mama's family—the Blackfoot—and ours.

"I've been thinking on what Preacher said," Jack said after a while. "And I think he's right that we need to be risktakers about trusting God. I think this land is worth the risk—that we're worth it, Callie. I know it's been hard, but when hasn't it? If you think about it, we've been risk-takers all along and didn't even know it. Jessie trampin' all the way west with nothin' but a bundle on her back . . . Quinn goin' it alone after losin' his whole family, and you and me losin' Pa and our sister, Rose, like we did." Jack glanced over at me and smiled a wry kind of smile. "And I think Lillie took the greatest risk of all, marrying me . . . "

"Not so big a risk as you think," I said, feeling the love in my heart swell for my brother. He smiled.

"You know what John-Charles told Lillie today?" he asked then, and when I shook my head, he chuckled. "Well, you probably wouldn't guess it, but he told her that he didn't want her worryin' over him findin' out how his real mama died. He said he knew a long time ago that a bad man had shot her and that when the bad man went to shoot me, Lillie killed him. He said, 'Mama, you're a hero to me no matter what Mrs. Audrey says.'"

"How did he ever find out?" I asked through my tears.

"He found the newspaper article," Jack said, shaking his head. "God sure has a way of working things out, don't he, sis? That's why I know he'll work out our troubles with the ranch, too. We just got to ask him."

Then Jack did something that surprised me. He asked if we could pray.

As we joined hands, I felt Jack's hand tighten around my own, and I remembered then all the times we had taken each other's hands as kids, through the good and the bad, and I couldn't help thinking there was a different feeling to the way he held on. Like he wasn't just making sure I was there with him, but that he was there for me, too.

"What are you all prayin' about, Pa?" John-Charles said, coming up just as we said amen.

"Why, your inheritance," Jack answered easily. John-Charles seemed to think on that a moment, then he took his hat off and wiped his brow tiredly.

"Well, can we just start with dinner? I'm awful hungry," he said, and we laughed.

Not long after we got the horse to the corral, I stood and watched Jack walk away with his son, his hand resting on John-Charles's head with such love. And for some reason I remembered a time on our old farm back in Missouri, watching Jack and Pa walking together in much the same way. I remember how Jack had looked at the ground as the afternoon sun glared down over them and then how he had looked back up to Pa.

"Pa, when do you think my shadow will be as big as yours?" he asked. And I recall Pa looking down at him with a soft smile, touching Jack's head as he did.

"Why, when you become a grown man—like me," Pa had said simply, and Jack had looked worried all of a sudden, like he wasn't sure if he would make it to being like Pa.

A worry he had carried in him over the years, I thought then, and I had the strongest urge to yell after him then, to tell him how much his shadow looked like Pa's now . . .

October 28, 1873 . . .

Another cold day. The sky is choked with heavy gray clouds that hang so low over the valley I feel like I could take a needle and stick it into them to make them rain . . . Instead, I'll be mending the mountainous stack of clothes sitting before me as I wait for another loaf of bread to come out of the oven . . . and there goes the poetry right out of me.

Quinn came in tonight, and I knew right off something was troubling him, whistling like he did while he helped Patrick carry in another load of wood. I had to ask a couple of times before he finally came out with it, sitting down at the table with a long sigh.

"Truth is, Jack and I are about at our wit's end. With Coy gone right now, we're short a hand—and we need the help more than ever with the cattle straying every which way to find grass," Quinn said tiredly, and I saw Patrick and Rose's eyes meet across the table, worried for their pa.

We joined hands then to pray over our dinner, and as

soon as we said amen Patrick reached over and touched Quinn's arm, patting it the same way I did his when he needed comfort.

"Don't worry, Pa," he said. "God's sure to send help, now. I told him while we were praying that in case he hadn't heard, you needed help and that I didn't think I'd ever heard you ask for anything in my whole life."

"Well, I'm not so sure that I haven't asked God for things," Quinn said with a slight smile on his face. "But it's a fine thing to pray for your family, Patrick."

"I prayed, too," Rose said, not to be outdone. "Patrick just said it first."

Mara Lee suddenly let out a yell right out of the blue, startling herself more than she did us, and we all started laughing. She looked toward each of us, unsure what to do for just a moment, then it occurred to her she already knew what to do—and she laughed.

Quinn laughed, too, leaning over to pull Rose and Patrick to him, hugging them as if to say it would all turn out fine. But tonight, just before he nodded off to sleep, I felt him search in the dark for my hand again, heard him sigh when he found it.

This time, though, it was me that whispered, "Everything is going to be fine."

It has started raining tonight as I'm writing this, the big drops of water hitting our roof like heavy drumbeats. I can't say how many times since we've been here that I've sat hearing that sound . . . but I can say I never get tired of listening. Sometimes I've even thought how good it would be to climb into the loft and lay on Rose's or Patrick's bed with a lamp and a good book and just escape from everything while it's raining like this. But I've never done it. Seems my only free time is spent with you, little journal, and I just can't bear to trade our visits for anything. Makes me think of Willa's pictures—I talk, you listen—but there's more to it than that . . .

There are times when I hear God's voice whisper to me as I put all these thoughts to paper, and those are the best times of all . . . Only right now, I keep hearing those words of Rose's, and it makes me wonder if he doesn't whisper to her, too.

Be of good courage, I hear. *I got you this far, didn't I?*

October 29, 1873 . . .

Rose has scared us nearly half to death today. It was around noon, when the men came in from rounding up more cattle, that I first noticed she was missing. I had looked up from setting the table and for some reason, it dawned on me that I hadn't seen her in a while. I could see Patrick and John-Charles with the men down at the barn, so I went out on the porch and called for her, then I went to Lillie and Jessie's cabins—but she wasn't there, either.

By the time Quinn came up to the cabin with Patrick, I was starting to get scared.

Quinn searched the barn and corral then joined Jack and John-Charles, riding out to search the pasture. Lillie, Jessie, and I searched all along the riverbanks. By that time, we were all hoarse from hollering for her and thinking the worst of what any parent can think might happen, what with the grizzlies and moose that lurk in the willows near the river this time of year . . . And just as we joined up back at the barn, Patrick showed up and confessed that he knew where she went.

"She rode off that way on Midnight," Patrick said, pointing away from town as all heads turned to him.

"Where, son?" Quinn said, his voice as breathless as I felt, and I knew he had seen the fear in Patrick's eyes, too.

"To the Norton place," Patrick said, and no sooner had he said it than Quinn was up in the saddle and heading out again, Jack not far behind. "She wanted it to be a surprise . . . she was going to find you some help, Pa," Patrick called after Quinn, but they were already gone.

Jack told us later that Quinn had rode straight up to the porch of the old, run-down house and that just as he was dismounting, they all saw Mr. Norton career out of a tall stand of weeds, a whiskey bottle in his hand. Before anyone could say anything, Quinn was inches from the man's face.

"Mr. Norton, you don't know me, so I'll get right to the point," Quinn said softly. "My name's Quinn McGregor, and my daughter, Rose, has turned up missing. The thought is she was headed this way."

"I might have seen her," Mr. Norton said, wiping his face with the back of his hand. Then he looked up, like he might have recalled some foggy memory. "She's a pretty little filly, right? With red hair?"

Something in the way the man said that set Jack's temper off, and he stepped in front of Quinn then, talking real quiet. "Now, my brother-in-law here is what you call a God-fearing man," he said. "Don't get me wrong. I fear

God—but I love my niece, too. Point is, *I* don't fear death
. . . But mister, I have a feeling you do. So if you know anything, you best tell us now."

It was about that same time that Rose and the Norton
boy came trotting up on their horses at *our* ranch.

Mercy took one look at the faces of Jessie, Lillie, and
me, then walked slowly over to where John-Charles and
Patrick stood. She tugged on John-Charles's trousers, and
when he glanced down she said, "I think we ought to pray
for Rose now."

Gale is the Norton boy's name. "But it's Gale like in a wind-
storm," he'd made sure to add, smiling a shy kind of smile at
me as he turned and shook everyone's hands so politely. As
I watched him, I couldn't help thinking there was something about him that was different, something almost gentle
in spite of his large build, that made me think he was more
the calm after the storm than anything else . . .

Later, after the men had calmed down enough to
decide to hire him and we were all in the kitchen getting
dinner ready, Rose told us she thought he didn't have the
nicest of parents, that they had been arguing real loud
when she had rode up to fetch him for Quinn. She said
that something had crashed against the wall just as Gale
had opened the door to her. She said Gale had just shut
the door, soft-like, behind him and walked slowly out to
the yard with her. And once they got away from the house,
he had unwrapped a kerchief of his and took out a handful
of toy soldiers and began lining them up on a stump—that

even when the yelling got real loud, he just calmly kept arranging the soldiers in neat little rows until he was satisfied with how he'd placed them.

When she asked him what he was doing, he looked up at her and said, "This is one game I can win."

"When we were riding back here, I asked what he wanted to be when he grows up, and you know what he said, Mama?" she said then, looking at me with a puzzled but kind of sad look to her pale blue eyes.

"He just said, 'Someone who cares.' He can't be a heathen and say something like that, can he, Mama?"

Rose didn't wait for my answer but shook her head and started in on kneading the bread for me. "No," I heard her say, real quiet, after a while. "I don't think he's a heathen at all. I just think he got stuck with heathens for folks."

I looked over then at Jessie, who had been listening while she worked, and I saw her wipe her hands across her apron. "Well, that may be the case as far as that boy's folks," Jessie told Rose. "But you're the one we almost died worryin' over today. Don't you go runnin' off ag'in like that and not tell us where you a-goin', sis, you hear?"

Rose smiled her best charming smile at Jessie as she worked at the dough. Then with a little flip of her head she said, "Oh, Jessie, don't you know I can handle myself? I don't need no one worryin' over me."

"Don't need no one, huh? Well, there ain't much brag in that, sis," Jessie replied. Then I heard her say it again, almost like a whisper, like she was deep in thought over something or other. "Don't need no one." But when I looked over at her, she just smiled and smoothed over her skirts, real prim, like I'd never seen her do before.

Lillie, who had been sitting in my rocker bouncing Mara

Lee on her knee, just looked up at me with one brow arched and said, "I'd hate to be on the other end of that thought."

It's been decided that Gale Norton will take over Coy's old place in the bunkhouse while he helps Quinn and Jack finish the roundup.

I think Jack has taken quite a liking to him, too. When I went down to the bunkhouse with some extra blankets for Gale, Jack was just leaving, and I noticed there was a look of amazement on his face.

"That boy's something else," Jack said, taking his hat off his head and worrying its brim with his fingers as he spoke. "I asked him if we should let his folks know where he was, and he said for me not to bother myself, that they probably wouldn't notice he was gone." Jack looked up at me and shook his head. "And he didn't even say it mean-like, either, sis—just said it like he was stating a fact. Then he told me he was willing to work hard for his keep. Said, 'Mr. Wade, I plan to be better than what I came from, and the way I see gettin' there is to work. So you can count on me workin' real hard for you and Mr. McGregor.'"

"Rose said his folks seemed rough," I said, suddenly wishing I had brought more than just blankets.

"Well, she was right about that," Jack said. "But he's different than them; I can tell you that already. You talk to him, and you'll see—he feels like family already," Jack said, smiling at me as he turned to make his way up to his cabin. "I think he might be one of them risktakers, too," he added, not bothering to look back.

I made my own kind of discovery in a way when I knocked

real light on the bunkhouse door and heard the boy's voice saying to come on in. First thing I saw was Gale sitting on the little bed of Coy's, his large frame hunched over as he read from the Bible by the dim light of a single lantern. Coy must have left the Bible behind. Then I saw Jasper lying curled up at the end of his bed . . . and Honey, who never lost any time deciding if she liked someone or not, was lying right on the bed with him, her head draped over his leg.

"Well, I see you got company," I said, offering him the blankets. He set down his Bible and smiled.

"Yes ma'am," he said, taking the blankets. "Do you know when her pups are due?" he asked then, taking me by such surprise that I sat down on the bed next to him, stroking Honey's fur as I looked her over.

"I *had* wondered at Honey filling out so much lately— and even had worried a little about her moving so slow, thinking she might be sick," I said, almost to myself. Then I looked over at him watching me with a pleased kind of smile, and I couldn't help but smile back. "But it never occurred to me that she might be with pups."

There was something about his eyes, I noticed then, that reminded me so much of Quinn when we first met. Not the color, for Quinn's are blue to Gale's brown, but the haunting look that was in them . . . along with the endurance it took to get past the pain.

"Looks like you're going to have some company, then," I said. He laughed outright, and Jasper and Honey both barked, too.

"I don't mind the company," he said, patting them both on their heads. "I'm glad they're here."

I thought on what he said all the way up to the house—

and how really glad he looked to be there in that little bunkhouse with just a lantern and two dogs. It made me wonder just what kind of life he had lived with those folks of his.

A *risktaker*, Jack called him, *just like us* . . .

I know Isaiah himself said your ways are unsearchable to us, Lord, but I don't think it would take much searching even for me to see that you have sent this boy to us . . .

October 30, 1873 . . .

It's a dark, cold morning.

Rose is back to working on her sampler again. Quinn says she is to work on it until she learns to be a proper-acting young lady. Not long after he closed the door behind him and Patrick, Rose looked over at me with a forlorn look on her little face and said, "Well, how long is that going to take?"

Quinn killed an elk this afternoon after they had finished a day of "rounding up the ladies" . . . a good thing, going into the winter months, knowing we will have the extra meat. And it seems hiring Gale has been another good thing. Quinn told me tonight that the boy worked as hard or harder as he and Jack and that he never complained.

"He acted as if that meal you packed him to take along was the best gift he ever had," Quinn said, shaking his head.

"Maybe it was," I said, and when our eyes met, it was

like we were both wondering what kind of gifts Gale Norton had ever got from his parents, if any at all.

I'm glad he is here . . . so is everyone else, judging by the steady procession that has gone to the bunkhouse since he came. Jessie gave him one of Stem's old overcoats and some trousers as well and demanded Gale's old worn-out pair so she could mend them. Lillie took him some more blankets then went back with some jerky and a fresh pitcher of milk, "just in case," then looked put out that I had already thought of the milk.

"Well, I don't know what all the fuss is about," Rose said as we were getting dinner ready—still grouchy over her imprisonment. "He's just come to help with the roundup."

"Maybe," Jessie said, planting her hands on her hips. "But your ma and pa, your Uncle Jack and Aunt Lillie— even me, sis—we all know what it's like not to have nobody. An' truth is, *ever'body* needs somebody. Like I told ya before, there ain't much brag in sayin' otherwise."

"Yes ma'am," Rose said, ducking her head as tears filled her eyes. I saw the anguish in her eyes of once again being put in her place by Jessie—*Jessie, who had always favored her so!* But Mercy was quick to sidle up to Rose, patting her on the back.

"It's all right, Rose," she said softly. "I know you're not *really* bad."

At least Rose had the good sense to look contrite when Gale came to join us for dinner with a little wood carving of Midnight he had done for her.

Me, Jessie, and Lillie grinned amongst ourselves; we knew Rose didn't mean what she said. She had been making over Gale along with the rest of the children. But it doesn't hurt to let her chew on a little piece of humble pie, either . . .

Jasper and Honey are going crazy outside as Quinn drags the elk to the barn, barking and doing zigzags around him, hopping like rabbits, making me smile.

I'm surprised Honey can manage, fat little bug that she is now . . .

October 31, 1873 . . .

Cold again today . . . or maybe more chilly than cold but *that* will come soon enough. Rose watches out the window as the men ride out. Mara Lee sits on the floor, slapping the tin plates I've given her to play with. Sometimes I wish I could turn back time, and Rose would be Mara Lee's age again. When I confessed that to Quinn this morning he said, "What would you do different? Make her not *Rose?*" I told him I couldn't bear that, either . . . and he smiled and kissed my nose. But I *do* worry over her reckless ways sometimes. I don't understand why she takes off like she does, not telling anyone where she's going. Going off on a whim to fetch the Norton boy wasn't the first time, and my heart of hearts tells me it won't be the last . . .

I have to stop this, have to put Rose in the Lord's hands just as I've promised to put all of my other worries and fears.

Take care of her, Father. Talk to that heart of hers and show her your way . . . she means an awful lot to me.

Patrick came in tonight nearly beside himself with excitement as he told us how Gale is showing him and

John-Charles how to carve figures out of little pieces of wood.

Rose appeared unmoved, but the bother showed true in her eyes. Patrick, with ways that are beginning to remind me so much of his father, was quick to sense her hurt.

"Don't be sour plums, Rose," Patrick said softly as he sat down next to her on the couch and leaned his dark, wavy head against hers. "You'll be carving with us soon enough."

Quinn and I both glanced over at each other questioningly—then we both grinned as it dawned on both of us at the same time what he had meant to say.

Grapes or plums, Rose seems to have been gentled by her brother's love tonight, and I know I have you to thank for that, Lord.

November 1, 1873 . . .

So much for Rose staying gentled for long . . .

We had a hard enough day as it was, the men being so cold and weary from driving the rest of the cattle in, that the rest of us pitched in to get just a bit of the cut hay to them. By the time we finished, we were all dirty and tired. I guess I was too tired to think, because when Rose asked if she could "please just ride Midnight so she can stretch her legs a little," I didn't see the harm in it.

I should have known better. I think down deep I did, especially when I saw Gale speaking to her before she rode off and saw Rose wave him off with a little flip of her hand. Yes, I suspicioned something then, but it wasn't until the rain started that I noticed she hadn't made it back.

"I told her she shouldn't go so far, that it might rain," Gale said with a frustrated but worried sound to his voice.

And it was Gale who first spotted her coming down the slope in the rain, looking as relieved as I felt. We all leaned forward, squinting from the porch, catching only a glimpse of her going into the barn as a flash of lightning struck: no bonnet on, her long hair plastered to her back as she swung off of Midnight.

"Never knew a child to take off like she does—except for maybe your brother," Lillie said, smiling wryly at me as she released the breath she had been holding in. "I guess I spent so many years praying for a real home, I figured to stick to it once I got it."

"She wasn't hurting anything," John-Charles said, real quiet, always Rose's defender when push came to shove. Patrick looked at him like he shouldn't say any more, then Mercy, who was standing between the two of them, tugged on their trousers to get their attention. Patrick looked down and said, "I know, I know. Let's pray for Rose."

As aggravated at Rose as I was for scaring me again, I sent her to fetch some milk for dinner in spite of her being drenched. Rose gave me a pathetic look, then turned and shuffled back out the door without another word.

It wasn't long after Rose left that Jessie mumbled something about forgetting something down at her place, that she'd be right back. I was just about finished with dinner when I heard the most awful, blood-curdling scream come from somewhere outside the cabin. Quinn and I were up and running out the door with everyone else on our heels.

The rain had stopped, and we found Rose lying crumpled not too far from the barn, her face a mask of terror as she looked up into Quinn's and my eyes.

"A big man!" she croaked out as she took another great gulp of air. "He tried to *take* me!"

"Pa, look over there," John-Charles said softly, and when I saw Jack start off in the direction John-Charles pointed, I went, too. Jack whispered something about there being a big man out there lurking in the shadows and if I was going to be fool-headed enough to follow, I ought to at least stay behind him.

But it wasn't until we were almost upon the "big man" that I realized it was not a man at all—but Jessie wearing Stem's old hat as she skirted along the edge of the brush toward her own cabin, carrying a thick bundle under her arm.

"Jessie Dawson!" I hissed under my breath, and she started. Then she grinned, shifting the bundle of men's clothes to her other arm.

"Guess our sis might not be so headstrong no more 'bout handlin' herself," Jessie said with satisfaction. "Guess she might just figure she *does* need folks around that cares."

Jack burst out laughing. "I swear, Jess," he said. "I think I would've sworn off cards sooner if you'd been around to set me straight."

"I'd'a cured you from a lot more'n cards, Jack," Jessie said, wry-like, and we all laughed, heading back down to the cabin.

Rose, of course, played the perfect victim to Mercy as she hovered over her, wiping the tears from her face with a cloth. But it was Jessie who held her hand, murmuring in all the right places as Rose told her about the huge man that had dragged her behind the brush, "very nearly taking my life," Rose said, her eyes becoming as round as saucers as she looked from Patrick to John-Charles to Mercy, then finally to Gale, declaring she'd never doubt Jessie again "as long as I live."

"Well, that's an awful long time to be making such an oath, sis," Jessie said. "I think if you jes concentrate on *now*, you'd be doin' good."

"Oh no, Jessie," Rose declared solemnly. "I think I ought to stick with *as long as I live*. Just to be on the safe side."

"Well, who can argue with that?" Jessie said with a satisfied note to her voice, and we all couldn't help but smile—even Gale, who is new to our little flock but seems to feel as much exasperation over Rose as the rest of us.

Everyone is asleep now but me. Quinn is just the opposite, saying he would have to sleep on it before he could think of what we should do about Rose. But I find myself unable to rest, thinking of what she said when I saw her off to bed, when I asked her why she did the things she did . . .

"I don't know why, Mama," she whispered miserably, staring up at me with those huge eyes of hers. "It's like when I hop on Midnight and ride out, I go on an adventure in my mind, and I forget the time." She looked like she might cry at any moment, so I sat down next to her and hugged her to me. She buried her face in my neck, like she used to do when she was smaller, and she poured out her sorries into my neck. She sobbed that she was sorry about hurting me and Quinn . . . sorry for making Jessie cross with her.

She pulled back from me not long after that and looked up into my face, like she was trying to decide if she should say any more. "Sometimes I worry that all of those adventures

I read about folks doing in books . . . that there won't be any adventures left by the time I get old enough to do them," she confessed. "I even prayed and asked God to keep some on hold for me."

I brushed my hands down the length of her still-damp hair, over and over again, trying to figure out what to say to my sweet, reckless daughter, but all I could think of to tell her was that I loved her . . .

I was wrong, little journal. It isn't Patrick who favors Jack when he was young. Rose has become so restless, so impatient with life lately, that she reminds me more and more of Jack, with her "I got to do it my way" and her eyes that always search the distance for something none of the rest of us can see . . .

Lord, I pray to you for the wisdom to handle this the way you see fit. Because right now I feel useless to know what to do.

And that's about the worst feeling I think a mother can ever feel . . .

November 2, 1873 . . .

Sabbath morning . . . Just me and Mara Lee again. I've become grateful for these mornings I spend alone with her, grateful for the way she looks up into my eyes with such happy trust that I feel like I must be doing something right . . .

There is a thick frost covering the windows; winter is breathing its first breath on our lives again.

With Preacher gone again, we decided to hold "church" at our cabin, filling it to the brim as everyone crowded in, shivering from the cold.

After we finished praying, Quinn opened the Bible, but instead of reading the Scripture like he usually did, he leaned over, pointing to the place he had marked, and asked Rose to read it. I was so glad he did and grateful, too—grateful to you, Lord, for leading him in that way.

He had picked a passage from the Book of Ephesians, and I thought I knew why as Rose began to read, her voice becoming more and more strained as she read the words before her.

"'Children, obey your parents in the Lord, for this is right. Honour thy father and mother; which is the first commandment with promise: that it may be well with thee, and thou mayest live long on the earth.'"

Rose paused then, thinking she was finished, and I admit, I did, too. But Quinn gently prodded her to go on. "'And, ye fathers, provoke not your children to wrath: but bring them up in the nurture and admonition of the Lord,'" she read, and then Quinn put his hand on her arm tenderly for her to stop reading.

"I would like to say something to my children now," Quinn said, looking around the room, and everyone waited, wondering, like I was, what he was about to say.

"I believe with all my heart that every word of the Lord is true. And in knowing that, I can keep the hope that my and your mama's dreams for you come true—that his promise comes true, that all *will* be well with your lives . . . and that you may live long and happy upon this earth."

Quinn glanced down at his large, work-worn hands then, and there was such a humbleness in the way he looked that it brought tears to my eyes. When he looked up, I saw there were tears in his eyes, too. "Rose, Patrick," he said quietly, "I hope that I've not provoked either of you to wrath . . . and that I've done as the Lord has asked and trained you up in his ways. If I have done anything wrong, I want to right it, because I love you . . . and I don't want you to lose that promise."

"Oh, Pa," Rose said, her voice barely a whisper, "you've never done *nothin'* wrong."

"Never," Patrick echoed. Then he and Rose looked at each other as if they couldn't imagine anyone saying that *their* pa had done anything wrong—most of all, to them.

I could tell those thoughts stayed with the two of them throughout the day . . . as Quinn's words stayed with the rest of us. Lillie was the first to speak of it, though, as she took Mara Lee from me so I could make a fresh pot of coffee.

"I wish I'd had a Pa like him, Callie, when I was growing up," she said out of the blue, and then another voice said, "I do, too," and we turned around to see Gale standing there, holding Mercy's hand. I caught a brief look of bittersweet longing on his face, and then it was gone, replaced so quick by a smile that I wondered if I had imagined the look.

"I guess we've all been orphans a time or two in our lives," Jessie said, rising from her chair then, and I saw her glance Gale's way before turning back to us. "That's why the Lord put us together *now*. So we could see what real family is all about."

I am so thankful we did witness what real family is all about today, Lord. A real family with you in it . . .

Quinn had done what any good father would do: He had put the burden upon himself, allowing his children to see the truth through humbleness and love.

But he did it because he trusted you, God. Without even realizing it, Quinn did the same as Jesus in that scripture Preacher read to us: He humbled himself and became obedient . . .

I pray we all can become more like that, Lord—more like you each day we walk through this sometimes troublesome but beautiful gift you've given us called life.

November 3, 1873 . . .

Back to work on this cold, cold morning. I've baked two loaves of bread, mended Patrick's pants yet another time, and heated the last pan of water to finish scrubbing the floors—although now I'm wondering about the wisdom of that; it's just begun to sleet outside, a fine mist coming to us in sheets through the gaps in the mountains. Already I can see where the muddied footprints will land . . .

Patrick did bring in enough wood this morning (aided by Rose, no less) before they all left to go help set out hay for the cattle. I think he and Rose are bent on proving to Quinn their wayward ways are not his doing—especially Rose. I've never seen her throw herself into housework with such eagerness—making beds, changing Mara Lee for me while I finished cooking breakfast. She even made the trip down to the bunkhouse to fetch Gale when it was ready. She really is a sweet little girl.

And Patrick, with the way he held his "Bird" in his arms nearly all through breakfast, just to see if he could make her laugh. They've only been gone a little while, and I miss them, miss Quinn . . .

Never mind the muddy footprints; I hope they come in soon.

Mara Lee is pounding on the rail of her crib, hollering with her newfound voice. I think if she could talk, she would say she misses them, too.

November 5, 1873 . . .

The warm Chinook wind that came in sometime last night has brought us beautiful weather. Some call it Indian summer—*why* I'm not exactly sure, but it seems to have brought the "natives" out to the ranch today to celebrate.

Peach was the first to show up, and by then we had already made up our minds to make a day of it, the general thought being that it would probably be one of the last times to enjoy the outdoors until next spring.

"I thought when I saw the sun shinin' like it was this mornin' there might be some shenanigans goin' on over here," he said. Then he took a second look as Gale came strolling out of the bunkhouse and added, "Guess I thought right," and we all laughed. Then we set about fixing what we could for our noon meal. Jessie brought a fine batch of biscuits she had just made, and Lillie the beans and some pickles she'd canned last summer, while I provided coffee and fresh chunks of elk the men roasted on sticks over a fire. It wasn't long after we'd started to set up our makeshift table that Preacher and Willa showed up.

We had such a good time of it, visiting and laughing, and I told Preacher as much as we watched the men start to set up the horseshoes.

"Always laugh when you can," Preacher said, grinning. "It is—"

"Cheap medicine," Gale finished, and we turned around. Willa's mouth dropped open as she looked from Gale back to Preacher.

"Did you hear that, Shawn?" Willa said, knowing full well he did, for he was standing right next to her. The humor of it wasn't lost on Preacher, either, as I watched him grin down at his pretty fiancée.

"Byron, wasn't it?" Preacher said, but Willa had turned back to look at Gale with a surprised but pleased look on her face, delighted to find such a "diamond in the rough."

"Quoting Byron," she said, smiling at Gale fondly. "I hope you like books as much as I'm guessing you do because first chance I get, I'm bringing you a stack from my own library. No sense letting a mind like that go to waste."

"I'd appreciate that a lot, ma'am," Gale said, smiling back at Willa like he couldn't believe what was happening to him.

None of the rest of us were surprised—Gale had gained more than a few admirers among us along the way as well.

Soon enough, the wind picked up, and we were heading back indoors, laughing again to hear the children beg Peach to take his teeth out for them again, which he did, to their delight—and it wasn't too much longer after that, that Peach came into the kitchen asking us if we had seen his teeth.

It seemed with all of their "funnin" around, poor Peach had forgot to put his teeth back in, and when he finally remembered, they were gone.

Well, we searched and searched all over the cabin, outside, then back in the cabin again . . . until we heard a horrified scream come from Mercy and went running to see what was the matter.

Mercy was standing stock-still, staring in horror at her stuffed bear sitting on his usual place of honor on the settee—a spot that we had passed back and forth more times than I could count during our frantic search. Our eyes followed to where Mercy's shaking finger pointed, and that's when we saw Peach's false teeth, grinning madly from the bear's mouth . . . and suddenly John-Charles was nowhere to be found.

Peach was the first to talk. He took one look at the bear and said, "Dern, them teeth look better on him than me!" and whatever we had thought to do to the culprit was lost then in our fit of laughter.

It was Rose who cornered John-Charles later, just before they were leaving for the evening.

"Admit you did it," she said, perching her hands on her hips.

"Did what?" he said in that quiet way of his, but as they squared off to outstare each other I saw John-Charles start to waver. First his eyes, then I saw his lip curve into what might have been a smile. Rose grinned triumphantly.

"I knew you did it," she said and flounced off with Mercy.

"How did she do that?" I heard John-Charles ask Patrick then, and I saw Gale ease closer, too, as if he was hoping for Patrick to shed some light on Rose's mysterious ways as well.

"I haven't figured it out, yet," Patrick admitted. "But it helps if you don't look at her."

Such a good day, all and all, Lord. And so good to see Preacher and Willa again. He says he will be in town for this next Sabbath, and we're all tickled about that.

Willa, I think most of all.

November 6, 1873 . . .

I read another Bible story to the children tonight. Since Gale has never attended one of our little get-togethers, we let him choose. So it was Daniel and the lion's den again— one of their favorites.

The story, much to my surprise, went off without a hitch, most likely because they were all so tired . . . But I should have known the evening's entertainment wasn't over when I watched Patrick suddenly rise from the floor and stroll over to the window to look out.

"Looks like Old Man Winter is comin'," he said, his voice lower than I'd ever heard, and when I realized he was trying to be like Quinn, I had to bite the inside of my cheek to keep from grinning. Then Mercy was suddenly standing next to him, golden curls tossed messily around her wide, innocent face as she took a glance out the window, too.

"Old Man . . . like Peach?" she asked, turning to look at Patrick. When he nodded yes, she clutched her bear to her chest protectively. Patrick caught the move and looked over to where John-Charles sat and grinned.

"Yeah, like Peach," he said, and Mercy looked thoughtful for a moment then turned to look back out the window. But I noticed the ever so slight move of her hand as she covered her bear's mouth.

"Well," she said finally, "I'm gonna pray Old Man Winter has his own teeth."

Funny. I just came in from outside; I do smell snow in the air tonight. I used to think Mama was fooling us when she'd lift her nose to the wind and declare that she could smell rain or snow coming. But then, when I think about it, there were a lot of things she said when I was young that I doubted.

I wonder if Patrick and Rose doubt some of the things I say. I wonder if one day they'll say, "If only I knew then what I know now."

Probably. Who was it that said youth was wasted on the young? I can't remember his name, but I think he was right . . .

November 7, 1873 . . .

So cold today, bitterly cold—enough to take your breath away, is more like it—and now, after what's happened tonight, it's as if I feel that bitterness came to steal the peace in my heart away as well . . .

I can't remember what time it was, but I know it was late, for all the children were already asleep when Gale came to the door to tell Quinn and me that Honey had had her pups. I knew there was more by the look in his eyes—Quinn did, too, and it was a moment before Gale could tell us he wasn't sure they were going to make it.

As soon as we were inside the bunkhouse, I could hear Honey's tail start to slowly thump against the floor, as if she sensed we were there to help her. But sadly, there was no helping three of the six pups, who were already dead by the time Quinn picked them up to examine them.

It might sound silly to some, but the look in Honey's big eyes as Quinn took three of her puppies away from her nearly undid me. I wanted to say something, but couldn't find the words; feeling another's sadness like I do, has always turned me silent that way.

"'Twould probably be best if we didn't mention these little ones to the others," Quinn said to Gale, and he nodded his agreement, but I saw the hurt of it in his eyes, too.

"Have you ever wondered why stuff like this happens?" Gale said then, avoiding my eyes. "I mean, why did they have to die? Why *couldn't* they have just lived?"

"More times than you know," I said, nodding and finally finding my voice. "And I haven't gotten an answer yet."

Quinn glanced up at me then, and when our eyes met, it was with an unspoken understanding of two people who had been through those questions together over the years.

It was when Quinn went to go bury the pups that I suddenly felt the overwhelming urge to get away. Without a word to anyone, I grabbed up his old overcoat, went down to the barn, and saddled up the buckskin. I don't remember thinking about anything as I did it, and I can't really explain it now as I write this . . . But all I knew was that I had to get away . . . from Honey's sad eyes and Gale's questions . . . So I rode. I rode and rode . . . the only other time I remember riding like that was when I was just a girl, when we were on the trail coming west. I remember riding out with Jack to see my first glimpse of the Platte River and the endless stretch of land beyond it, and I remember, too, how much it scared me. The bigness of it all . . .

But this time I realized I wasn't scared but searching— as I dismounted on the crest of the upper slope leading to the mountains.

The moon was so full and bright that it almost didn't look real. It resembled a huge, shiny coin some great hand had set down in the middle of the picture . . . almost too big and so close that it made even the mountains look small. It made me realize how small we really are compared to all of God's creation. I think it amazed me, too, to think how much he cared in spite of that . . . and suddenly I knew then that all the tumbling and turmoil in my heart that I was trying to sort through, to explain, he already knew.

"I wish I knew the whys of things," I whispered up into the huge bowl of night sky filled with stars. "But more than anything, I wish I knew you better . . . "

And no sooner than those words were out of my mouth, I felt a strong but gentle voice say to my heart, *You will.*

I wish I could put to paper how I felt up there, just me, standing underneath all that majesty but suddenly feeling more a part of it than lost to it . . .

I don't know how long I stood there like that, but after a while, I heard footsteps coming and turned to see Quinn leading his horse and looking more than relieved.

"It's a good thing for the full moon and this frost," he said. "Otherwise I wouldn't have been able to find you."

"I don't know why I ran off like I did," I said, trying to find the words to explain. "It's not as if I haven't seen animals die before."

"What you saw was a mother lose her young, something all parents fear," Quinn said gently as he came to stand next to me, and it amazed me again, even after all these years, how well he knew my heart . . . sometimes, I thought, better than I did myself.

"You scared me, you know," he whispered into my hair finally, and I let him pull me close.

"I can take care of myself, you know," I said in half-hearted defiance. Quinn turned me around, taking hold of my chin as he looked into my eyes.

"So you can," he whispered, an amused look in his eyes, and it hit me then how very much I sounded like Rose.

"I sounded just like Rose then, didn't I?" I said, and he chuckled and took my hand as we turned to walk the horses the rest of the way down the slope together.

"Yes, you did," he said. "I expect that's part of the reason I love her so much."

We walked hand in hand like that all the way back to the cabin, and I can't help thinking even as I write this that my dear friend Grace was right in what she told me all those years ago about me and Quinn.

I think her words were, "God knew what he was doing

when he put you two together. One day you'll see the truth of that, too."

So I do, old friend. So I do.

—Early morning with Mara Lee again, and I just came across this scripture: "Be of good courage, and he shall strengthen thine heart"—Psalm 27:14.

And you have, Lord.

PART TWO

Tearing Down the Walls

So after Joshua took his shoes off, God told them to GO FORTH, march around the city SEVEN TIMES and holler like crazy at the Enemy. And when they did what God said, the walls came down and they were all pretty happy about that.

By Rose McGregor
Almost 14
Montana Territory, 1873

November 9, 1873 . . .

Sometimes I think Preacher would have made a fine writer. Not that he's missed his calling, because he hasn't . . . he just has a way of telling things that makes it stay in your mind long after you leave. It's like reading a book that's so good you not only can't put it down but have to keep opening it back up to read it again. Today was proof of that, for I keep turning my mind back to the words Preacher spoke to us . . .

By the time we got to "church," the tent was already packed to overflowing. I spotted Willa, who had saved us a seat with her somewhere in the middle of the mass of people, and as I struggled with the rest of our brood toward her, I could feel something different in the tent.

Preacher even seemed different, the way he walked to the front of the tent with such a determined look on his strong face . . . like God had put something on his heart and there would be no rest for him until he told it. I saw him glance toward us and smile, his eyes even lighting up a bit at seeing Gale with us. He bowed his head, then said a quick prayer, and started right in to talking.

"As I was praying this past week, the one thing the Lord kept putting in my heart was to remember that the strength we need to get through the trials in our lives isn't our own, but his," Preacher said as he looked around the tent full of faces. "He got my attention on that one; I have a pretty strong hunch he knows what he's talking about when it comes to battles."

Everyone chuckled then, and Preacher smiled good-naturedly and went on.

"Well, you know, if you think about it, Joshua didn't do what he did on his own strength. Rahab didn't do what she did on her own strength . . . and neither did King David. Does anyone remember what David said to Goliath just before he slew him? 'Thou comest to me with a sword, and with a spear, and with a shield: but I come to thee in the name of the LORD of hosts, . . . for the battle is the LORD's.' Three very different people—Joshua, Rahab, and David—but the one thing they had in common was their faith in God, not in themselves. They believed that with God by their side they could defeat their enemies, and they could take the land God had promised them.

"Now, I know some of you might be thinking you can't compare yourselves to folks from the *Bible* . . . but that's just what the Lord wants you to do. He wants you to remember these were just plain folks: Joshua was just a poor kid without a home. Rahab, well, we all know what she was. And David? A shepherd boy, the youngest and smallest of the bunch. But all three of them knew they could make a difference in their lives by letting God's light shine *through* them."

Preacher paused for a moment, and as he did, I turned and looked at Gale, who was watching and listening as if his very life depended on it. Quinn looked, too, then turned back to smile at me.

"There was a great artist I happened upon while I was in Boston," Preacher said. "I'm not going to mention his name because, well, that's not important. But I want to tell you his story because in a way, it's our story, too."

I saw a lot of folks lean forward then when Preacher said the word *story*, for he was known throughout the territory to be a fine storyteller.

"See, I heard from some of my friends that this artist

had created a real masterpiece," Preacher said, "and I got to thinking maybe I ought to see it for myself. So I went to this fellow's studio and asked if he would let me see it, and to my surprise he said yes. He ushered me into this room where a large painting stood on an easel, and I saw even from a distance that the painting was, well, good but pretty plain—just a landscape of rolling hills and trees with a small country church placed just in the distance. There was nothing grand about it, and it sure wasn't what I would call a masterpiece. To make matters worse, the closer I drew to that painting, the more I realized there was slashes and cuts all over that huge canvas."

"Well, I stood there thinking, *What in the world has he done to his painting?* Finally, I turned to him and said, 'Sir, did you know there is what looks to be knife cuts all over your painting?'"

Preacher paused again and leaned against his little podium. "Well, that fellow just smiled at me and real casual-like, he walked over to the windows of his studio and started pulling back the heavy drapes like nothing had happened. By this time, I pretty much figured the man was crazy. But then he joined me again, standing by my side, and we both watched as the light began to pour through those slashes that I had spotted.

"Suddenly, I saw that light fill the painted hillsides, sweeping the grass here and there with warmth as it moved slowly toward the church in the distance. Then I saw the light hit the tall steeple, illuminating a gold cross at the top that I hadn't even realized was there before. Folks, that painting had become beautiful to me and so real that I felt I could step right into it and be at that place.

"'You see,' the artist told me then, 'those slashes are

how the light gets in. Once it begins to work its way through those cuts, it is able to illuminate the painting. The *light* is the key because it fills the gaps in with its beauty . . . making my creation more beautiful than it would have ever been on its own.'"

Preacher looked around the tent again, and when he did, I could have swore I saw tears standing in his eyes. I glanced over at Willa, and she looked teary-eyed, too, but as eager to hear the end as the rest of us.

"I can't tell you how many times I've thought about that artist and the freedom he had to look at his work as only half-done without the light. My prayer for each one of you today is that you can see your own life with the same eyes as that artist. That with every one of life's cuts, you open yourself to God's light. Because the more we allow God in, the more his beauty, his strength are able to shine through wounds and heal them . . . once and for all."

Preacher went to step down then, but something else seemed to occur to him, and he held up his hand to get our attention.

"If you can't remember anything else from today, remember this: Jesus said, 'My strength is made perfect in *weakness.*' He was saying, 'I am shown strong in your weakness.' Let him be your strength, folks."

It was a quiet crowd that filed out after that. More, I think, because we were all thinking on what he had said . . . and how badly we did want God to fill those scars in our life with his light.

I know I was thinking it. And as I watched my family's faces—Jessie, Lillie, Jack, Quinn, and even Gale—as they took turns helping to bundle up the children and then slowly climbed into the wagons to head for home, I knew they were thinking it, too.

It's snowing again, harder, like it's serious about staying. I just got back from checking on Honey and her three little pups. They were all nestled in a blanket on Gale's bed, Gale on one side and Jasper on the other, like two sentinels keeping watch over them. Gale sat up quick when I came in, but he didn't leave Honey's side. It was the sweetness of his worry over her that caused me to reach out and start to brush the dark hair back from his forehead, just like I do with Patrick, but Gale flinched, like he thought I might strike him.

"I'm sorry," he said, looking embarrassed, and all of a sudden a peace came over me, and I knew it was God's love for the boy, because for once I knew just what to say.

"Sorry for what?" I said, smiling like nothing had happened out of the ordinary, and I saw the relief come quick to his eyes. We sat next to each other for a while like that, just petting Honey and looking at the pups. Finally, Gale set one of the pups down next to Honey and turned to me, a pensive look on his handsome, young face.

"Do you think Preacher was right about God healing our scars once and for all?" he asked quietly, and when I told him yes, he nodded again and seemed to go somewhere inside of himself, deep in thought.

"We all have scars, honey," I said, rising to leave so he could be alone in his thoughts. "It's just some's already been healed by God and some . . . well, he's just waiting for them to ask him to heal them . . .

I'll never forget the look in those brown eyes of his as I turned to leave . . . reminding me of that poem I read once:

> Thanks to the human heart
>   by which we live,
> Thanks to its tenderness,
>   its joys and fears;
> To me the meanest flower
>   that blows can give thoughts
>   that do often lie
>   too deep for tears . . .

Still waters run deep, my mama always used to say. I pray for that boy tonight, Father, that you reach out to him and let him know that you are waiting to heal his hurts . . . just as you have done for me more times than I could ever count . . .

November 10, 1873 . . .

I have to wonder at the timing of Preacher's message with Medicine Weasel and One Shot showing up here tonight, nearly froze to death and so sick—with what, we're not completely sure. But if Jessie's right about what they have, we're all going to need every bit of strength you can give us, Lord . . .

Rose had been out in the barn with Gale, seeing to a calf, when she heard riders coming and had run out to see who it was, delighted to recognize the visitors were her old friends Medicine Weasel and One Shot. It wasn't until she got right up on them that she realized they were bad sick.

"Scared me to pieces, Mama. They looked like dead men riding horses," she said breathlessly as she followed us all down to the bunkhouse, emptied of Gale and the pups the minute we found out the sick men had come to stay awhile. Quinn lifted One Shot out of his saddle and carried him easy as a baby into the bunkhouse as Jack helped Medicine Weasel down from his horse and half-carried him, too.

"No, Rosie," Jack said gently as Rose tried to follow him in. "You can't come in here until we find out what's wrong with them. You keep John-Charles back for me, too, you hear? He's going to put up a fight once he finds out his grandpa is here. And you're the only one I know who can help with that."

Rose nodded, taking her new duty seriously as she planted herself outside the door while the rest of us went in.

It wasn't until Quinn turned up the lantern that we got a good look, and never a more pitiful sight have I seen in my life. Medicine Weasel, who we had seen only a year ago, was just a shell of what he had been before, his long hair, stringy and nearly all white now, stuck to the sides of his gaunt face in clumps, and One Shot, who was just as gaunt, looked as if he had aged twenty years.

Medicine Weasel, as he warmed up under the blankets Jessie had thrown over him, finally came around just enough to talk to Jack, switching from Blackfoot to English the best he could with his tongue swollen so bad.

He told Jack that the reservation had become a "death camp," that the American traders dealt mostly in whiskey. He said after a round of trading, if the braves, drunk on whiskey, didn't freeze to death before they reached their lodges, they would be quarreling or killing one another once they got there. He said it was a bad place and that he and One Shot decided it was time to leave.

"I don't fear death, Jack Wade, as much as I do life now," Medicine Weasel said in his sad, lilting English—then promptly passed out, shocking us all.

"He's burning up with fever," Jack said worriedly as he felt the old man's head and looked over at Jessie. She pulled their covers away for a moment and lifted both of their shirts, revealing a horrible-looking rash.

"Lord, have mercy on us all," Jessie whispered, straightening the blankets back over the men after she had looked both men over. She glanced to Jack, then me and Quinn. "Those fellows got the scarlet fever."

Never in my life have I felt such a cold fear grip me, hearing those words. I saw the fear in everyone's eyes as we quietly went about making our old friends as comfortable as possible, then turned to retreat to our own cabins . . . to our families . . . and wait it out.

Wait? *Wait for what?* my mind wants to shout tonight. For the doctor who will never come? For someone else to stand over them and declare them sick?

Remind me, Lord, who I am. Remind me that you are here with us. And that, like Preacher says, you are shown strong through our weaknesses.

November 11, 1873 . . .

Snow's falling heavy on the roof this morning. I don't like its sound, like a weight settling down over us all, as much as I do the sound of the rain . . .

I almost had a moment's peace while I was rocking

Mara Lee, but when I looked down into her face, the question suddenly went through me: *I wonder if she'll get the fever.* Then it was, *I wonder if Rose already has it . . . or Patrick . . . or Quinn . . .* The list rambled on through my mind until I pulled out my Bible and began to pray . . .

Lillie, Jessie, and I waved to each other from a distance this afternoon as we went about our chores. Earlier, we had talked of what to do if one of us starts to show the sickness, and it started sounding insane. We should move little Mara Lee to Jack and Lillie's . . . No, Jack had been in there with Medicine Weasel and One Shot. To Jessie's, then. No, Jessie had been with the sick ones, too. *And so had Quinn and I . . .* So we do what we have no other choice but to do: We wait.

I feel as if I'm back standing on that slope, looking at the immense moon that dwarfs everything else around it . . . only it's not the moon but the words *scarlet fever* that hang over us, and this time I'm not awed. I'm scared.

I can see John-Charles down in front of the bunkhouse this evening. On and off through the slanting sheets of snow, he paces back and forth, reminding me of a wild horse that's been penned up. Only it's his grandfather and One Shot that's been penned . . .

Maybe he feels the same way, judging by the look on his face as he heads back in this direction after Jack and Jessie just sent him on his way. Lillie is waiting for him on the porch, and as she opens the door to their cabin, I can see Mercy is plastered to her side. I know Lillie must be sick with worry, as weak as Mercy's always been, being born early like she was. We're all worried—for the children more than anything. I can see Gale's eyes before me as I write this, and I can't imagine what he must be thinking . . . if he's wondering whether anyone is worried for him.

I need to go in. I just came out for a breath of air, and now my hands feel frozen solid.

Jessie came and talked to me from the porch tonight, shivering in spite of being bundled in Stem's old overcoat, but when I asked her to come in, she was having none of it. "I'm not sure if'n I have it, Callie," she said, her dark eyes kind but worried, "but I don't want t' make that sweet baby sick if'n I do." I handed her a cup of coffee as she told me that Medicine Weasel and One Shot seemed to be holding up but that they weren't out of the woods yet. She told me Jack looked tired, but he's not sick yet and neither was Gale, who seemed to be faring nicely down at her cabin. I asked her then how long it took for the sickness to show.

"Three days, mostly," she said, and by the way she studied my eyes I knew she had guessed that I had started counting down in my mind.

November 12, 1873 . . .

The snow just keeps piling up, forcing Jack and Jessie to use the ropes to drag their way through it down to the bunkhouse to nurse Medicine Weasel and One Shot.

Quinn and Gale go out to scatter hay for the cattle, who are bawling as pitifully as I feel. Rose is helping me bake bread this afternoon, chattering to Mara Lee as she kneads the dough, and I find myself glancing at her from time to time, wondering if her eyes look a little feverish. Patrick, who is always quick to sense how I'm feeling, has done the only thing he can think to do: bring in enough wood to build another cabin.

November 13, 1873 ...

We had just started thinking maybe we were out of the woods . . . that maybe none of us would get the fever, when Rose came into the living room after dinner with a look of fear on her little face.

"Mama, I don't feel so good," was all she said, but as soon as the words came out of her mouth, I felt my heart leap up into my throat. Quinn's eyes met mine, his fear mirroring my own; we'd heard about the worst cases— convulsions, blindness . . . even death. Of course, all anyone ever remembers about sicknesses is the bad.

"Pa, what's wrong with Rose?" Patrick asked as he looked up from bouncing Mara Lee on his knee. He must have seen the look of fear on Quinn's and my faces, for he stood then.

"Go fetch Jessie, lad," Quinn said quietly, and Patrick handed Mara Lee over to me and was out the door in a flash. Rose didn't show much fear at all until Jessie walked in the door, taking quick to Rose's side to help her up the stairs to the loft.

"I'm sorry, Jessie," Rose whispered pitifully, lying back on her bed. I saw her pick up her Stem doll and clutch it to her chest . . . saw her cheeks stained red by the beginnings of fever.

"Sorry about what, little sis?" Jessie asked, looking over her shoulder at me.

"I shoulda listened to you about taking off. But I did it again when I saw Medicine Weasel and One Shot. I didn't make it to 'for the rest of my life' like I said I would."

"None of us ever do, sis," Jessie said, her voice shaky with emotion as she gently tucked the covers up under Rose's chin. "None of us ever do."

Once I got the children down, I went in and lay next to Quinn for a little while, just until he dropped off to sleep. Even without words, we were thinking the same thing as we both searched for each other's hand in the dark . . . as we both sighed once we found it.

November 14, 1873 . . .

It's morning now, and I'm not sure if Rose is any better for my staying up with her or for the willow-bark tea I made her to try to ease the pain in her throat or the salve I rubbed over her little rash-covered body, but I can't *not* do something. Patrick complained of a headache and sore throat when he woke up, but Mara Lee seems fine, thank God; I've heard it's harder on the babies.

I just pulled those little yellow-hearted daisies Quinn gave me out of the pages here. "Tiny but tough," Quinn had said. But I'm not tough . . . I don't *want* to be . . . not without you, Lord.

I think Quinn's been thinking the same thoughts as me today. I found him down in the barn tonight, his broad shoulders hunched over as he sat on the cold, hard dirt floor, picking up Honey's pups out of the pile of blankets with such care, rubbing their coats dry with an old piece of cloth. Like he always has since we first met, he sensed me in the room before turning around.

"Don't know how these little ones got so wet, lass, but they're apt to catch their death if they don't get dry," he said, quiet, not looking up. "They're too little to do for themselves just yet."

"You've always done right by us, Quinn," I said gently, sensing his feelings. "Always fought for us."

"But I can't fight this sickness," he said finally, his voice hoarse, and I realized the mighty oak of a man we all depended on being strong had been hit by a storm he wasn't sure how to fight.

"It's not our fight," I heard myself say, remembering Preacher's words and with the memory, feeling a bit of strength come to me. "It's God's."

Quinn was silent then. But even in the dark of the barn, I saw the wheels turning in his mind, as if, if he thought hard enough, an answer would come. That's when I asked if he remembered Joseph of the Old Testament. I told him he'd always reminded me of Joseph: strong and honorable, never letting go of his beliefs no matter what happened. Then I reminded him how Joseph had stayed faithful—and when he did, God did, too.

"I wish I were really that strong, Callie," Quinn said,

soft, then turned his head to look at me. "Do you think it wrong to pray to be that faithful? To pray for that kind of strength?"

I didn't answer but just took his hand in mine and without another word, we knelt together in that dark, hay-filled barn, praying for all we were worth, like two orphans trying to find their way back home . . .

Quinn has finally dozed off, but I can't seem to find sleep. Sitting here writing all of this, I can't help thinking of how Quinn and I *are* orphans in a way, losing our parents as early as we did. I can't help feeling my heart ache with the wish to have Mama here by my side tonight . . . to tell me everything is going to be all right and hear the words of that song whisper through my mind:

> Backward, turn backward, O Time in your flight
> Make me a child again, just for tonight
> Mother, come back from the echoless shore.
> Take me again to your heart like before.
> Kiss from my forehead the furrows of care,
> Smooth the few silver threads out of my hair.
> Over my shoulder your loving watch keep—
> Rock me to sleep, Mother, rock me to sleep . . .

Better yet, let me be *your* child, Lord. Hold me in your embrace and let me hear that everything is going to be all right.

The Other Side of Jordan

Still no signs of Mara Lee being sick. Patrick seems to have recovered without suffering through much of the sickness at all, but my poor little Rose is worse, still suffering with a fever and headache. And now her tongue has swollen, making it nearly impossible for her to talk and tell me what she needs. When she looked up at me with those pale blue, innocent eyes of hers, I felt the helplessness of it go through me like a sharp pain. By the time Jessie came to check on us, it was all I could do not to throw myself in her large, comforting arms and cry.

Jessie didn't seem to notice my distress at first, busying herself with spooning some more tea into Rose, telling us that it seemed John-Charles had weathered the fever much like Patrick, and Mercy didn't have it at all . . . and that Gale, sweet boy that he is, had been doing Jack's share of the work and his, too, with Jack helping to nurse Medicine Weasel and One Shot, then coming back to Jessie's cabin at night to make little carvings for the children. It was only when Jessie and I had sat down in the kitchen for coffee that I finally gave in to my feelings and told her I was scared.

"Sometimes it seems no matter how hard I try, I can't shake my fears," I blurted out. "It's like I almost get there, then something else happens."

Jessie set down her coffee and wrapped her arms around me again, in just the way I imagined.

"*Almost* is human . . . it's jes what we are, honey," she said, pulling back finally to look at me with a kind look in her old, dark eyes. "Ya jes got to let go and let God. When ya *really* let go, that's when ya start seein' *his* work in your life, and there ain't no better beauty than that."

She smiled at me then, and told me to rest a spell. "I got a story to tell ya," she said. "I ain't the fine talker Preacher is, but I reckon I kin help ya see what I'm tryin' t' say." She went on to tell me then that back at the plantation, where she'd lived as a girl, there were weavers. She said once she got old enough, her mama started teaching her how to weave. One of the best lessons her mama told her before she got sold off was about the weaving.

"We'd always leave a flaw in our work; Mama said it was 'out of respect for God'—an' most of the time, we didn't even have to try, neither," she chuckled. "But one day I'd made a fine rug, not a flaw in it, and I wanted it t' stay that way. But I knew my mama was gonna tell me about it, too. So I went to her first and asked why. She said, 'Jessie, reason *why*, is to remind ourselves that no matter how hard we try in this life, only the good Lord is *perfect*—and that anything that even comes close to that in our lives is because his hand be in it.'"

Jessie leaned back against her chair and looked at me with love.

"That feller Preacher spoke of them holes cut in that painting of his'n—that was the same idea. He saw that his work was just that: work—till he let God's light shine through it. That's when it became a . . . what did Preacher call it?"

"A masterpiece?" I said, and she smiled a pleased smile.

"Yes ma'am, that's the word I was looking for: *master-piece*. I kindly like t' imagine that's what the good Lord be doin' right, now . . . standin' back and waitin' till he can see all his light shinin' through." Jessie leaned forward and patted my hand softly, then she whispered, "Then he kin call *us* his masterpiece."

I told Quinn tonight about what Jessie had said, and he nodded then sat quiet for a while, stoking the fireplace with more wood as I finished nursing Mara Lee. He was so tired . . . I could see it in his eyes: the days of working with Gale and Patrick, trying to keep the cattle from starving or from freezing to death in the snow that never seemed to end. But when he turned back to look at me, I saw the endurance in his eyes, too.

"I think we should pray, lass," he said, and I laid Mara Lee down and joined him, dropping to my knees beside him on the little braided rug in front of the fireplace.

"Father," he began, his deep voice bringing me comfort, "Callie and me, we want to give you *all* of our lives. Not just the parts we can think of to give, but all that we are . . ." He cleared his throat then, and I felt his hand tighten over mine. "We want to give you our trust again . . . our faith . . . to open our hearts to your mercy for us and for our children."

We prayed for everyone then: for Rose, for Jack and John-Charles, for Medicine Weasel and One Shot, for Lillie, who had welcomed the Blackfoot in like they were her family. We prayed for Jessie, who had once again set aside her worries for her own family who hadn't come home yet, so she could help us . . . and for Peach not to be alone anymore. Then we prayed for Willa and Preacher, that they be kept safe and that Willa would be able to trust God, too, for Preacher's safety while he was away. As the prayers were starting to trail off, I felt something in the room had changed, almost like a fresh breath of air had just blown through the house. I know Quinn felt it, too, for he said, "In Jesus' holy name, we pray these things." Then he turned to look at me with tears in his eyes.

We smiled at each other, then we both said amen together.

November 16, 1873 . . .

It seems the whole world was praying with us last night— or at least a goodly part of Montana—and I can't think of a better day to hear such things than on the Sabbath. Lillie was the first to come to the door this morning to tell me she couldn't handle being away anymore and to say that she had felt led to pray last night and had even prayed for *Mrs. Audrey and her family!* Then Jessie came in with the news that she and Gale had had "church" at her cabin, too. But it was when Preacher and Willa showed up with some news of their own that stunned us the most.

Willa joined us in the kitchen, barely taking a breath before telling us that she had been holed up in town, taking care of Preacher, who had come down with the fever, too. She said she was doctoring Preacher when it hit her that Preacher didn't have to go out of town for something to happen to him. She said it was like a voice came to her heart all of a sudden and said, *You have got to learn to trust me, Willa. You have learned how to survive, but you haven't learned how to live again.*

Willa looked at all of us with great tears in her eyes. "I dropped to my knees right then and started praying. I told God I was sorry. I told him that I didn't know as much as Shawn does as far as the Good Book goes, but I remembered the part where Jesus said he was coming to give us life so that we could live it more abundantly. I said I figured I had insulted him and his Son, living like I didn't know that, and then I asked him for his help."

Willa smiled wryly then. "Shawn opened his eyes right after that and looked at me, kneeling by his bed, and he *grinned* at me. "He said, 'Willa, that was some fine sermonizing you just did. But don't get in your head that you can take my job. You've already taken my heart. Besides, I'm feeling much better now.'"

We all laughed, and when our laughter had died down a bit Lillie happened to ask Willa if she knew anything of the Audreys.

Willa's smile dropped a bit then. "Yes, they're in a bad way with the fever, too, both of them so sick they can't tend to themselves. And their girls are sick, too," she said, shaking her head sadly. "Mrs. Audrey hasn't ever been much of a friend, but I wouldn't wish scarlet fever on my worst enemy."

Lillie got a real thoughtful look on her face then, but before I could ask her what she was thinking, she said she had to go check on Mercy and John-Charles.

It wasn't until later, after I had looked in on Rose again and packed up some food for the men working outside, that I found out what had crossed Lillie's mind. She came back by the cabin to tell me that she was going to take a trip to town . . . that Jack knew about it, and she wanted me and Jessie to watch out after John-Charles and Mercy.

"What in the world are you going to town for?" I asked, shocked, and Lillie looked at first like she didn't want to tell me, but then she did.

"John-Charles isn't sick anymore, Callie," she began. "And Mercy, thank God, she didn't get the fever at all. But I started thinking this afternoon that if she had gotten it, I would have had all the help in the world . . . " She hesitated, then looked at me straight in the eye. "Which is why I've decided to be the one to go to the Audreys, to help with their girls that are sick."

I started to protest, but she held up her hand. "They don't have *anyone*. Willa said Mrs. Pumphrey and Widow Spence are down with it, too." Lillie smiled bravely, and I saw something light in her eyes then, like she realized that all the months of Mrs. Audrey making her feel like she was less than nothing were meaningless when it came to times like these . . . that maybe she had a lot more than she ever thought.

I helped her bundle up, and as we walked out to the wagon, decked out with sled runners that Gale had readied for her, I saw her seem to gather strength inside of herself with each step. We said a quick prayer together, and when it was finished, I saw God's love shining clear in Lillie's eyes.

"It doesn't matter anymore what she said, Callie," she said quietly. "What matters is what I do . . . especially knowing what I know in my heart about Jesus. Because I know if it was me, if it was my babies . . . I know he'd tell someone to come to us. And I hope that there would be enough of him in that person that she would listen, too."

As Gale and I watched her leave, I felt him turn to look at me with a thoughtful look on his face.

"John-Charles was right about his mama, Miss Callie," he said, turning to look back at the wagon fading quick into the distance. "She is kind of a hero, isn't she?"

Willa was as surprised as I was with the news when I came back inside and told her.

"Well, doesn't that beat all, Lillie tending to her tormentor's kids," Willa said, shaking her head with a strange kind of smile on her face. "Who would've ever thought?" She looked out the window then, drying the dishes with a thoughtful look on her face. "'God is a comedian playing to an audience too afraid to laugh,'" she recited softly before turning back to look at me. "I remember reading that once, and I can't help thinking of it now. It's almost funny, but I'm not going to laugh—not just yet, anyhow. I figure I just got in his good grace; I don't want to get out."

We smiled at each other.

"I learned a long time ago that God has a sense of humor," I said. "I figure that's why we do, too, being made in his image like we are. The thing is, you never can tell what he's going to do next . . . or just how he'll work things out."

"Isn't that the truth!" Willa said, sighing. Then she looked up at me with a grin. "I think we ought to sit back and watch the show, don't you?"

"I guess we should," I said chuckling with her in spite of myself.

Later—

Rose seems to be on the mend, and I have no one but you to thank for that, Lord. Thank you for everything you've shown me these past couple of days. I was wrong when I said youth was wasted on the young. I'm starting to think the older I get, the better I get at living this life you gave me.

November 17, 1873 . . .

The sun is back out like bright yellow fingers that reach through the gaps in the mountains to peek into the snowy valley. Rose is faring better today and even sat up to take some broth I made her, whispering she loved me in a raspy little voice . . . Patrick is outside again with Quinn, Gale, and the cattle . . . always the cattle. Mara Lee slaps her tin pans to some wordless beat, making Mercy laugh.

It's John-Charles I'm concerned about. Ever since Lillie left for town, he's been trying his best to get into the bunkhouse and see Medicine Weasel and One Shot. Jack told me today that One Shot seemed to be getting better but that he wasn't so sure about Medicine Weasel.

I'm going to go down there tonight and see if I can help in any way.

I just came back in from my visit to the bunkhouse. Medicine Weasel seems a little better, now—so do Jack and John-Charles . . .

I admit when we first walked in I thought for sure

Medicine Weasel was already dead. One Shot took one look at us and nodded politely, as if it was the most natural thing in the world for his friend to be lying next to him, dead, then went back to flipping through the pages of a book Gale had left.

Jack gave a worried look John-Charles's way, then walked slow steps over to the side of Medicine Weasel's cot, leaning down to check his breathing. He must have seen something, for the next thing he did was shake Medicine Weasel.

"Don't you think about dyin' on me, old man," Jack said, more his fear talking than anything.

Medicine Weasel finally groaned, slowly opening his eyes to look at Jack.

"I wish you wouldn't have woke me, Jack Wade," the old man said. "I think by the way everything looked, I was almost home."

Jack started to say something back to that, but Medicine Weasel waved his gnarled old hand as if to quiet him, then he rolled his head my way.

"Tell me, what does Grandfather say in his Book about someone who is alive but feels dead?" he asked me. "I feel like I have a lot more dead pieces in me than live ones."

I said a quick prayer to myself and then went on to tell him there was still hope. I said that we all die, little by little, each day because of the craziness in the world.

"But if we ask God to take the dead pieces out of us, he will," I said, thinking of Preacher's and Jessie's stories. "Then he can replace them with new ones of his own."

Medicine Weasel nodded thoughtfully. "This might be a good thing," he said, then he turned to Jack. "But you know, when I was going home, I don't think I felt those dead pieces."

"Well, you can't go yet," Jack said. "Your grandson needs you."

John-Charles must have felt it was safe for him to step out from the shadows then, for he did and quickly walked over to the side of his grandfather's cot. "Grandfather," was all he said. But I saw Medicine Weasel's eyes light up then, like something had sparked in his spirit, and I sensed the old man hadn't felt needed in a very long time.

Medicine Weasel struggled to sit up then, and as he did, he glanced out the door of the bunkhouse then turned back to John-Charles.

"Do you think you could help me get my lodge set up when I get well?" he asked, and John-Charles promised him he would.

The old man nodded then gave a great sigh, as if he had made his decision.

"I guess I won't die today," he said, smiling softly as he leaned back against his pillow and drifted back to sleep.

Sitting here writing this, I can't honestly say who was more relieved with that old man's decision to live: Jack, John-Charles, or me . . .

November 18, 1873 . . .

Rose's beautiful long hair is coming out by the handfuls now. Jessie says it's because of the high fever, that she's seen it happen before. It just breaks my heart, and I know Rose is hurt, too, but she is trying to put on a brave front for me.

"At least I can talk again, Mama," she said with a tired little smile as I tied a little kerchief around her head for her. But when I got down to the kitchen again to start dinner, I could have sworn I heard her muffled crying from up in the loft.

I think Mercy heard it, too, for she looked at me then scampered up the ladder, and she's been up there for quite a while now as I write this . . .

I am so tired tonight but thought to put down this scripture that I found earlier: "Hope deferred maketh the heart sick: but when the desire cometh, it is a tree of life"—Proverbs 13:12.

I think I know what it means . . . God gives us hope so we don't grow weary in our desire to reach out to him . . . and to find him is to find the tree of life.

Just my thoughts. I'll have to ask Preacher about it sometime.

November 19, 1873 . . .

Another sunny day but still so very cold. Jasper and Honey are on parade as I write this, strutting across the snowy yard, three chubby little pups with snowy faces trotting along behind them. Rose and Mercy have their faces pressed against the window, laughing as they watch. I see Rose reach out and touch Mercy's golden curls with longing, then Mercy throws her arms around Rose's neck, hugging her for all she's worth. Such sweet girls . . . they have grown so close lately with Lillie gone. Jack says she should be back anytime now after getting word that the Audreys made it through . . . I wonder what kind of story Lillie will have to tell . . .

I best close this book for now. Mara Lee is hollering indignantly, sounding much more like a *hawk* than a little bird . . .

November 20, 1873 . . .

Wonders will never cease with this family. But I guess it wouldn't feel like *my* family if something wasn't happening around here. I had just come back from the barn with Jessie and Willa, each of us with a pup in tow to show Rose, when we came into the cabin to find Mercy . . . without any hair.

I remember standing there, holding the puppies in shock, then looking down at Jasper and Honey as if they could shed some light as to what happened. Jasper and Honey looked from Rose to Mercy then to me, their large eyes seeming to wonder if my hair was the next to go. Jessie and Willa took the pups then and quickly made their way to the kitchen . . . I'm thinking, to hide.

"Mercy Wade, what have you done?" I said, finally finding my voice. But Mercy just stared over her shoulder at me with those large green eyes that seemed to see right into my soul.

"I told her not to, Mama," Rose said from the couch. "But she said Jesus told her to."

"What's that supposed to mean?" I asked, looking to Mercy again, but she just shrugged, taking Rose's hand in her own, patting it like a little mother. Finally she said,

"He just didn't want Rose to feel sad because I had hair and she didn't. So I cut mine." She looked back at Rose and smiled a sweet smile. "Now we're the same again."

I felt all the aggravation drain out of me then as I looked at Mercy's little head, now covered with nothing but choppy stubble. Then I remembered the first time I saw her, so small and fragile, brought into the world by love, the miracle of mercy allowing her to stay with us . . . And it made me think that maybe the mercy wasn't for her, but for us. And that she had somehow come to earth knowing a lot more about love than most people would in their whole lives.

Mercy turned and looked back over her shoulder at me then cocked her head to one side with a small, curious smile, like she was wondering what I was thinking. I went over and sat with her and Rose on the couch.

"You know, I was just thinking about that night I first held you in my arms, the very first night we met," I said to Mercy, and she smiled. "I remember kissing your cheek and whispering for you to fight for all you were worth. But what I won't ever forget is the look you gave me, like I could hear you speaking to me before you even knew how to talk."

"What did I say?" she asked, all eyes, and Rose leaned forward, too.

"You said, *It's you I'll be teaching how to fight, Aunt Callie,*" I said, and Rose grinned at Mercy, who was looking down at her fragile little body like she couldn't imagine it—not realizing yet the giant heart that beat within her and how much it was worth.

"And you know what else?" I said, swallowing past the lump in my throat. "I think God knew just what he was doing when he gave you to us. Because we're a better family for having you with us."

It wasn't until I felt a draft that I turned to see Lillie standing in the door of the cabin. Mercy raced over to her, oblivious to what she had done, and Lillie hugged her to herself, then stood up and inspected her head, which still had patches of hair in some places and nearly bald spots in others.

"Well," she said slowly, "it looks like I'll have to tidy up that work of yours a little, honey. You go on home, now, and I'll be along soon enough . . . "

Mercy gave an excited little wave to Rose, then was out the door. Lillie turned to me, a soft smile on her face.

"You know, sometimes I wonder if her spirit wasn't eavesdropping on my thoughts while I was carrying her; she's everything I hoped and prayed for myself to be . . . "

"Do you remember that ol' preacher's wife I spoke of, the one who got so vexed with me on the trail?" I said then, and Lillie looked at me with a curious smile.

"Della?" she said. "Wasn't that her name?"

I nodded.

"Yes, Della Koch. "'Blood will tell,' is what she was forever saying to me." I looked at Lillie and thought of how brave she'd been to go to the Audreys, of how much of God's love she had in her heart for others, and I smiled. "You know what? I think now is the only time in my life I couldn't agree with her more."

"Yes ma'am, Mercy's blood do tell," Jessie said, coming out of the kitchen with Willa—and thinking nothing of eavesdropping either, now that I think of it.

Lillie smiled then. "You know, the one thing I remember Preacher saying was that once we become Christians, we all become one family. So that would mean we all have the same bloodline now, wouldn't it?"

I will never forget the feeling in that room when our eyes all met and how we looked at each other with such love and gratefulness.

"Well, will you look at Mara Lee," Willa said as she handed her over to me. And just as we all leaned in to look at her, Mara Lee's eyes widened, and she looked past us, up toward the ceiling. Then she laughed like she'd never seen anything so beautiful in her life.

Suddenly it felt like a warm, heavy stillness had settled down over us, and I had the strangest feeling that Jesus had decided to join our little circle of exes—the ex-lady dealer, the ex-slave, the ex-divorcée . . . and, of course, the ex-coward—and I heard those words of Scripture come to me then, the ones that say everyone who loves is born of God and knows God. I think if I could have heard anything else right then, it would have been God's laughter, joining in with Mara Lee's.

November 23, 1873 . . .

Sabbath. But there will be no church—at least not in town, as Preacher is still too weak. But he asked Willa to bring over a Scripture passage he felt sure we were to have. If there was ever any doubt that God walks with our Preacher, well . . . those folks should read the paper he sent to us. Here's what it says:

> For ye have not received the spirit of bondage again
> to fear; but ye have received the Spirit of adoption,
> whereby we cry, Abba, Father. The Spirit itself

beareth witness with our spirit, that we are children of God: And if children, then heirs; heirs of God, and joint heirs with Christ.—Romans 8:15–17

As soon as Jessie finished reading that scripture, she looked up at all of us—but especially at Gale. They both smiled at each other.

"Makes a person think God whispers right into Preacher's ear, don't it?" she asked, but all any of us could do was nod.

As we all stood there, listening to Mercy's sweet little voice begin to rise up in prayer, thanking God for all he had done for us, for all the healings and the laughter, for bringing her mama home safe, I suddenly could have sworn that I heard Mrs. Audrey's words sweep through my mind again: *What a perfect bunch of outcasts*, she had said. But then I noticed something as I looked at Medicine Weasel and One Shot with their heads bowed so humbly . . . at Gale holding on to Rose's hand while Quinn held the other . . . at Patrick holding on to Mara Lee with such love . . . and at Jessie standing in between Jack and Lillie. I looked at those familiar faces and saw such love and thankfulness that suddenly those words didn't matter much anymore. And I noticed something else, too.

Somehow in the rush to join hands to pray, we had made a perfect circle.

PART THREE

Possessing the
Land

So the people took what God said was theirs all along, and God was pretty happy they finally did that. But them kings weren't. They tried to take every-thing away. DON'T WORRY, God said, I WILL MAKE THEM LAY UNDER YOUR FOOT. And he did.

I think God was just sick and tired of them messing with Joshua and the people.

By Rose McGregor
Almost 14
Montana Territory, 1873

November 24, 1873 . . .

There is a wind that blows through here today that is nothing like I've ever experienced before. It's as if everything it touches is made to look up and to try and reach out to grasp hold of it somehow. I see it as I watch the branches of the trees, bare but stretching their arms to the sky, welcoming it into our valley . . . in the way the horses toss their heads side to side, letting it ruffle through their manes. Quinn calls it a *new wind*, and I admit that's what it feels like. Like something new has come calling.

We first felt it when we bundled up and stepped out onto the porch this morning to drink our coffee together before the children stirred. It felt so good for us to be alone together like that, too, watching the sun start to rise up over the mountains . . . not really talking but saying more with our eyes than anything we had said before. It felt like our hearts were saying, *We've come a long way together, but there's still such a wonderful journey ahead of us.* That's when I first felt the stirring of the wind. Quinn felt it, too.

He kind of cocked his head to one side and smiled. "Do ya feel that, lass?" he said, and then he shook his head. "I've never felt such a mild wind this time of year. I wonder if it's what I've heard called a *new wind* . . . "

We watched the cattle trot across the lower end of the valley then, nosing their way through what was left of the hay that had been laid out the night before, and I asked Quinn if he thought they would make it to market.

"Next year we'll take them to market," he said, looking at them, looking at the land. "That'll give them the summer to fatten up on our grasses."

I don't know how to explain it, but there was something in the way he said that—*next year* and *our grasses*—that rang true to me. For the first time in a long time I had no doubt there *would* be a next year . . . or that our grass would return. And I didn't doubt that God had given us this land.

"Next year, then," I said, and as soon as I did, I had the oddest feeling that in the saying of those three words, somewhere out there our names had been stamped upon the land.

"Next year," Quinn echoed. Then he looked over at me and smiled.

I just turned to this scripture when I came in to write this: "Turn you to the strong hold, ye prisoners of hope: even today do I declare that I will render double unto thee"— Zechariah 9:12

Prisoners of hope? I can't imagine a better thing to be a prisoner of, than hope . . .

Later—

Patrick told us tonight that he has thought it over and figures we are about the best ma and pa he's "ever knowed of."

"I've thought that for a long time, too," Rose said, looking up from playing with Mara Lee. Then she looked over at her brother with a mixture I can only describe as love and endurance. "He just said it before I could."

Quinn and I grinned at each other, and Mara Lee picked that time to let out a yell that would have made Medicine Weasel proud, and we all laughed.

It's funny how in the middle of winter, I can feel in my heart like summer has suddenly come.

November 26, 1873 . . .

It's turned colder yet today, but everyone's spirits are up in spite of it, with Thanksgiving only a day away.

Medicine Weasel and One Shot watch intently from the bunkhouse this morning as Jack teaches John-Charles the finer points of setting up a Blackfoot lodge. Jasper is hopping up and down, that little rabbit hop he does, then he makes a grab for Jack's hat and runs for it. Jack yells, "Patrick!" and everyone laughs, most of all Patrick, who has been teaching Jasper how to snatch hats off men's heads if they forget to take them off when they come in the door . . .

I can hear Lillie laughing, too; she must be watching from somewhere on her porch. She still hasn't said much about her stay at the Audreys', other than that she did what she was meant to do and that Mr. Audrey and the twins were more than thankful. Jessie and I have wondered about that . . . but we've decided not to press her on it. She'll talk if she wants to. In the meantime, I'm just glad she's home.

So is Mercy. The sweet little thing is staying over to help Rose make the nut taffy for tomorrow; they chatter like magpies in the kitchen with their matching kerchiefs snug on their heads, Mercy lining the buttered pans with hickory-nut hearts while Rose pours the boiled maple sugar over them.

"This is hard work, Rose," Mercy says gravely.

"Well, what you can't duck, you best welcome—that's what Mama always says, anyway," I hear Rose say with a great sigh. And I can't help but grin as I write this and wonder if my mama smiled when she first heard me quoting her . . .

I hope so.

November 27, 1873 . . .

Thanksgiving Day and no one up yet but me and the turkey—and if he had a choice, I think the poor thing would up and walk out on me after the abuse I've put him through. Plunged into a pot of scalding water shortly after Quinn shot him out of a tree, then had his feathers plucked off, then rolled in a piece of paper and set on fire to singe off any fuzz, then rinsed. Next I wound up his legs with strips of cloth dipped in lard . . . I laugh as I read Mama's last instruction written on the faded and folded paper. She wrote it when I was just a girl not much older than Rose is now: "And don't forget to cook it, Callie!"

Later—

Well, thanks to Mama and a lot of other hard workers, our Thanksgiving has been a wonderful one. The turkey turned out real good, but the company was even better.

Peach was the first to roll in, and it tickled us to see he was all right after the scarlet fever scare. He was grinning ear to ear, holding a pan of green-corn pudding he had made himself that looked so good it shocked me to silence. Peach looked almost as good, like he had taken about ten years off his age, as clean as he was. Jack, being Jack, said, "Why, Peach, I thought you were against takin' a full scrub. Didn't you say you were afraid of going deaf?" to which Peach said, "I guess I decided I'd rather be deaf than lonely. And deaf would be a good thing if I had to stick around you very long!"

We all laughed then and turned to see Jessie marching in with Gale, carrying a fresh pan of johnnycakes—or ash cakes, as she likes to call them—setting them on the table next to Lillie's raspberry shrubs. Then Preacher and Willa arrived with several quart jars of her harvest cider that everyone loves so. Medicine Weasel and One Shot just stood back in a corner of the room and watched the commotion with a kind of dazed expression on their faces. But they were more than eager to take a seat when we told them dinner was ready.

I admit the question went through me then, wondering if they'd had much in the way of food before coming here. I think Preacher was thinking the same thing as he glanced to the two of them then sat down next to Willa. As we all joined hands, he said, "What's that old saying? It's a shame that it takes a poor man to remind you how rich you are." He looked around the table at us then cleared his throat. "Before we say grace, I was thinking maybe each of us should give thanks for all the things God's blessed us with in our lives."

We all agreed that was a fine idea and went around the table then, saying what blessings God had brought to us . . . all but Peach, that is. I think we all would have probably just let it go if it hadn't been for Mercy's persistence.

"Peach, ain't you going to say how God blessed you?" Mercy asked, her green eyes looking even larger as she blinked up at him from under the kerchief that had slipped low on her forehead. I saw Peach was fit to be tied to have to tell her no. "Peach?" she said again, and he took a big sigh then said kind of shaky, "*If'n* yer up there, Lord, I thank ya fer this family and fer makin' me feel like I belong somewheres. Because I reckon I ain't felt like that in a long time . . . if'n ever."

Quinn and I looked up at each other at the same time, touched by the old trapper's honest words—we all were. But it was Gale who appeared to be affected the most by what Peach said. I saw him look over at Peach thoughtfully, like he more than understood, but then he smiled and said amen, just like the rest of us. And like the rest of us, he had to blink several times . . . to get past the tears.

Such a good day . . . I don't think I've ever felt so much love or laughed so hard. Like Preacher says, laughter is cheap medicine—cheap but good—and I'm thinking the children couldn't have agreed with that saying more, the way they were carrying on this evening.

"Patrick, what did you say your blessing was again?" Rose asked for some reason tonight as they all sat in front of the fireplace. I saw Patrick side-glance over at her, as if trying to figure out what she was up to.

If the question was asked in innocence, we'll never know, because Patrick, so used to Rose setting him up for some sort of fall, finally said, "I said I was blessed for havin' Mama and Pa and you and Bird with me and that if I didn't ever have anything else that was OK because you's was enough." He rushed on before she could speak. "*And* you didn't mean to say that, either. Because I just thought it up and that's *why* I said it first." He smiled, satisfied, then added, "You ol' rag-head, you."

I said, "Patrick!" but all of them had busted into a fit of giggles—including Rose, who looked over at me with a grin after she had composed herself somewhat.

"Oh, Mama," she said, "that *was* funny. So that means it's OK to say." She glanced over at her brother and grinned again. "Ain't nothin' that beats a good laugh." But never to be outdone she added, "You ol' brush-head."

They all burst into another round of laughter at that— even Gale, who kind of shook his head, looking at Rose like she was the most curious but interesting creature he'd ever met.

I can't help but agree—and there *isn't* anything that beats a good laugh. Especially when you hear it ringing out of all those you love . . . like music.

I do thank you, Lord, for the sweet blessings of this day . . . for bringing us all through the sickness and for helping us to look forward again to what lies ahead. Although I do admit I have to fight the urge to glance up and say, "Can you give me a hint?"

November 30, 1873 . . .

The Sabbath bought us another trip to town, with Preacher feeling good enough to hold church now, even though he was still looking a little peaked—and he wasn't the only one. I noticed, glancing around, that there was quite a few folks in the tent that still looked a little pale. But there was a gladness about everyone, too; I saw it in the faces of my own family . . . in Willa's eyes as she looked at Preacher, even in the faces of Mrs. Pumphrey and Widow Spence . . . like stepping out onto your porch after a storm and seeing the sun again and just being so grateful you made it through the storm to see that sun.

When Preacher stepped up to start his sermon, I caught sight of the Audreys, too, and saw that same look on Mr. Audrey and the twin's faces. But Mrs. Audrey had a funny look to her, like she was trying to figure out a way to leave, but then Preacher started talking and I didn't have time to think on it, really, until now . . .

Anyway, the way Preacher looked around at all of us was so funny, almost like he was a little boy pleased to see his playmates had been able to make it over to play. "Well, I can honestly say I'm real glad to see we all made it here today," he said, earning chuckles from all around the tent. He smiled.

"The past few days I've been hearing a lot of stories from folks telling how God saw them through this sickness. One thing I realized was that each story was different, but the *how* of it was the same . . . because every one of you has said that you kept your eyes on the Lord."

Preacher cocked his head to one side and looked at us. "Do any of you remember what happened to Peter when he asked Jesus to call him out of the boat to walk on the water with him?" Preacher grinned. "Well, he walked on the water, of course." Everyone laughed, then Preacher's face grew sober. "But do you remember what happened when Peter took his gaze off of Jesus and looked down at those stormy waves? He started sinking . . .

"*That's* what I want to talk to you about today. I want to tell you that these kinds of trials will come, but if you can just keep your eyes fixed on Jesus, he will see you across those stormy waters. And if you just happen to look, you will see that he's walking through the storm with you."

A few people said amen, then it got quiet again.

"Listen, folks: Jesus walked through storms of life during his whole journey here on earth. He didn't care that he wasn't rich, that no one stood with a crown of jewels to place on his head. He didn't care that he was jeered at and heckled—even though he knew who he was . . . even though *heaven* knew.

"The one thing he *did* care about was people. Think about it: Everything he did was about people. About love and humbleness.

"The *King of kings* humbled himself to wash the dirty feet of men, to talk to a fallen woman who believed she was too far down to be lifted up, to comfort one who grieved for another. He saw us with such bittersweet sadness because we didn't quite understand the truth . . . didn't understand real love. *He* knew that nothing else mattered in this world. Nothing but helping us find our way *home*.

"Yes, heaven is our true home. But never mistake God's understanding for us while we are *here*. Never mistake his ways that even Isaiah said are unsearchable. God knows the true desires of our hearts because he put them there . . . And just as he knew the children of Israel needed a place to rest, a place to lay their heads as they journeyed through life, so he knows we need such a place, too.

"That's why I don't want you to give up. And he doesn't want you to give up, either. God has given us this place to call home; I have no doubt of that." Preacher looked over at Willa and smiled. "That's why I'm willing to press on. And my prayer is that you will, too.

"Listen: The Lord knows these trials will come; he knows all and sees all. And because he sees all, he also knows that joy will come again and so will the rest it brings. Our God, in all his wisdom, knows we couldn't bear the cruelty of the world without those moments, those seasons of joy. King David said he would have despaired had he not believed he would see 'the goodness of the LORD in the land of the living.' What's true of King David, who was called a man after God's own heart, is true of us as well.

"I ask you today not to give up—to have faith, to open your eyes, and to see that Jesus is there, walking right beside you. And if you want to remember any words this day, remember his, not mine. Remember what he promised: 'I will never leave thee, nor forsake thee.'"

"Those were some mighty fine words," Mrs. Pumphrey said behind me as we started to make our way out of the tent. I turned to see her and Widow Spence smiling kindly at me.

"Too bad there are those who don't seem to want to listen," Widow Spence said sadly, and they both glanced Mrs. Audrey's way for some reason.

The crowd surged forward, and all I could do was wave as I was led along with the rest heading in a hurry to their buggies and wagons. With it being as cold as it is, there would be no picnics after church until spring. Which is why we were all a bit surprised to find Peach slicked up again and standing just outside the tent.

He said hello to everyone, but it was clear he was nervous about something. Then I realized what it was as he chanced a glance over at Widow Spence, who was heading away to her buggy. Lillie looked to Willa, then over at me and winked.

Jessie saw it, too.

"Well, Peach, did *you* hear anything good?" she said over her shoulder as she and Rose climbed into her old wagon.

"Mebbe a thing or two," Peach said offhandedly as he shuffled his feet and glanced toward Widow Spence again.

Jessie handed the reins to Rose, who after her bout of sickness was back in good graces, and Rose grinned like she knew it. Jessie shook her head, smiling, and turned back to Peach. "Yer off to a good start, Peach," she said then, "but yer goin' have t' do better than that if ya want t' land yerself a fine Christian lady."

We all chuckled, and as I climbed up in our own wagon, I caught Mrs. Pumphrey watching us all with a pleased smile on her face, and I knew she had heard. I knew, too, that before the hour was out, Widow Spence would be hearing all about it, and I wondered how Peach would handle that.

I recall glancing down at Mara Lee then, bundled so good that all I could see was her blue-gray eyes and her mouth as she blinked up at me once then grinned like she thought Peach would do just fine.

Later—

Preacher and Willa made a special trip out here after church to tell us that Willa's decided to start a Sunday school, and I never saw a more excited little bunch—even Gale, who is usually so serious. Rose was the only one who took the news with casual indifference.

"Oh, I remember goin' to Sunday school in Californy," Rose said, like she was old hat at it as she spun the top they were playing with.

"Did you like it?" Mercy asked, all eyes.

"Well," Rose said slowly, "all I remember about it was I couldn't read yet, and they wouldn't let me talk *at all*."

"That must have been bad for you," Mercy said in all seriousness, and we all couldn't help but laugh.

But it wasn't until we got the children all down for bed and the men had gone to the barn to look at the horses that we heard the real shocking news from Willa.

"I know I probably shouldn't talk, but I just don't understand it," she started, taking a glance over at Lillie, who was filling her coffee cup.

"It's about Mrs. Audrey," she said, and Lillie looked over with a kind of worried look on her face. "Percy came to Shawn after church and told him Mrs. Audrey's decided to leave town—and I mean, *leave*: Percy, the girls, everything. He said that ever since she came out of the fever she's been acting real restless, saying she needed to get away. Then today after church she says to him, 'It took me nearly dying to realize I want to have a life—and living here is not what I call life.'"

Willa went on. "So Shawn goes with Percy to try to talk to her, but she already has her buggy loaded and is heading out without so much as a good-bye to Percy or the girls." Willa shook her head. "Shawn said when he looked into her eyes, it was like there was nothing there but darkness.

Then she says to Shawn, 'Preacher, if God sees everything, why hasn't he seen me?' Then he said she laughed real mean and left not long after that."

We all watched Lillie sit down at the table with a heavy sigh. "She was acting that way when I was there, too," Lillie said sadly. "Last day I was there, I was in her room, trying to tidy it up, you know, and she just started saying the most hateful things. She said, 'So, you're not just a dealer but a nurse now, too? Well, you might think you know every-thing, Lillie Wade, but you don't know me.' Then she laughed real hard and said it again: 'You don't know me.'"

Lillie looked at all of us with tears in her eyes. "I didn't say anything because I thought I should maybe just pray for her first. I was just so sure that God wanted me there . . . "

We gathered around her then, like we always did with each other, patting her on the back and trying to comfort her. But we were so shocked about all we'd heard, I can't even remember if we said anything. It was Jessie who seemed to break the spell, brushing her old, callused hand over Lillie's long curls.

"You did right, chil'," she said. "You did jes what the good Lord tolt ya to do, and that's more than a lot of folks." Jessie looked at me and Willa, and I saw almost that same look come over her sweet face that I'd seen on Lillie's face the day she went to take care of the Audreys.

"Best thing we kin do right now is pray for them Audreys," Jessie said. "The good Lord will do the rest. He always does."

And because we knew the truth of that, all four of us got down on our knees in my tiny little kitchen and joined hands. And we prayed.

December 1, 1873 ...

I had the oddest dream last night. I dreamt I was standing in the road in the middle of town, and suddenly I saw Preacher, standing at his pulpit. But the pulpit was in the middle of the road, too, and Preacher was dressed in what looked to be a judge's robes. Then I turned and saw that Jessie was standing next to me. She didn't turn to look at me but just kept looking up to the sky and then she said, "Pray, and the good Lord will do the rest. He always does."

Then Preacher raised this huge judge's gavel he had in his hands, and he struck it down against the pulpit.

And that's when I woke up to find Mara Lee banging on her crib for all she was worth ...

Rose and Patrick finished their lessons and their chores and were leaving to meet the others down at the barn for a round with the pups just as Jessie came in this afternoon. She took the cup of coffee I offered her and said in a distracted kind of way, "Do you remember when they said they'd be back?"

"Before Christmas," I said, knowing she meant her children.

Jessie just nodded and said, "Well, I don't know why, but they have been on my mind so strong today, I feel jes like I kin reach out and touch them."

She stayed for a while, talking small talk with me as I bathed Mara Lee, but she left not long after that. I watched her from the porch as she made her way to her own cabin, still distracted and every once in a while, glancing to the road that leads into the ranch.

This has been a strange day, to say the least . . . and I didn't even get the chance to tell Jessie about my dream.

December 3, 1873 . . .

Well, Jessie's mothering instincts have not faded in spite of her children being full grown. They all showed up at the ranch early this morning full of good news about their search for land.

Jessie was beside herself with happiness, and we all grinned at each other as we watched her hug each one like there was no tomorrow. "I jes knew you all was nearin' me," Jessie said, laughing. "I *felt* it in these ol' bones of mine."

"Not so old, Mama," Jessie's oldest boy, Jonah, said with tears in his eyes as she hugged him. "Not so old."

We finally got them all ushered into our cabin, being that it was the closest out of the cold, and Medicine Weasel and One Shot followed the rest of the group right in, too, their eyes filled with curiosity over the happy little group. Jack says it's because they haven't seen many black people. Medicine Weasel was quick to sit down at the table with them to get a good view, just as Jessie's daughter Sara told us all how they had got caught in a snowstorm just northeast of us. She said they ended up taking shelter in a tiny cabin with an old trapper-fellow named . . . *Peach.*

We all started laughing, and Jessie shook her head, grinning. "The good Lord surely has a sense of humor," she said. "And that ol' coot didn't say a thing when we saw him, either."

Sara looked around at all of us and shook her regal head in a way that reminded me so much of Jessie I couldn't help wondering if she was what Jessie looked like young.

"Well, whoever he is, Mama, he sold us the land for our town," Sara said with a triumphant grin as she looked at our shocked faces. Medicine Weasel was the only one that looked merely thoughtful.

"You all look about as shocked as we did when he made the offer," Jonah said, his eyes crinkling with a smile. "We had just about given up—but I say *just*—because none of us wanted to come home to Mama without our land."

"It was all Mama's doin'," Rachel, Jessie's youngest, agreed. "She gave us a talkin' to that would have lit a fire under a snail."

Jessie chuckled, wiping the tears from her eyes. "Oh, now, I jes told ya to remember them daughters of Zelophehad that Preacher spoke of before," she said, her dark eyes widening innocently.

"Uh-huh. What you *said* was, 'Maybe you all ought to start thinkin' like them girls did instead of like some orphans without a pa,'" Sara supplied. "You said them girls knew their *real* Pa—and knew they was good enough to step up to Moses and claim the right to their land. You said we'd be fools not to do the same—'cause we ain't orphans. The good Lord knows our names sure *enough*."

Jonah and Rachel chuckled with their sister.

"Why, Jessie, I never knew you could sermonize like that," I said, grinning.

"I think she could give Preacher a run for his money," Quinn added, and Jessie sniffed, folding her arms across her ample bosom in a perfect imitation of Rose.

"Might be I could do jes *that*," she said with a haughty air that made us laugh again. Not too much longer after that, we saw Gale walk in. He skirted around the tumble of children in the living room then stopped in the entry way to the kitchen, looking slightly amazed at all the new people in the room.

"Come on in, Gale Norton," Jessie said with a grin a mile wide. "You got some more family to meet."

I read to everyone the story of the daughters of Zelophehad tonight as Jessie and her family crowded in around the fireplace in our front room, read how these daughters who had lost their whole family in the wilderness had enough courage to go before Moses himself to claim their right to their father's and brother's inheritance. Then I read how Moses brought their case before the Lord:

"'And the LORD spake to Moses, saying: "The daughters of Zelophehad speak right,"'" I read to them. "'Thou shalt surely give them a possession of an inheritance among their father's brethren; and thou shalt cause the inheritance of their father to pass unto them.'"

"God did that cause they were risktakers, didn't he, Pa?" John-Charles said then, surprising us all, and Jack smiled at his son with pride.

"Why, yes, I believe so, son," he said.

"And because the Lord ain't no *suspector* of persons," Jessie added. "A very good friend of mine told me that awhile back, and I've found it to be true."

"I know who that friend was! That friend was *me*,

wasn't it, Jessie," Rose said sleepily, looking up from where her head had been resting on Jessie's lap. Jessie chuckled softly and patted Rose's little turbaned head.

"Yes, little sis," she said, "that friend was you."

Rachel stood then and took out a worn scrap of paper and read to us all what they planned to put in the newspaper to invite others to come to their town. I copied it down here so I could always have it to remember:

To the Colored Citizens
of the United States:

We, the company of the Town of Justice, are now in possession of our lands and the Town Site of Justice, which is located just east of Livingston, Montana Territory, and are happy to say it is the finest country we ever did see. The soil is rich, black, sandy loam, and the valley is eye pleasing, too.

We have secured the service of Mr. Coy Harper, a man of energy and ability, to survey and locate our colony. Now is the time to come secure your home in the Town of Justice, Montana Territory.

Not quite 90 days ago we secured our charter to locate the town site of Justice, and it has been by the grace of our God that come spring we will begin to permanently settle on our land.

Join us. Don't delay.

As soon as Rachel finished reading the announcement, we all clapped, and she grinned, glancing over to Jessie with tears of such love in her eyes.

"Why did you pick the name Justice?" Gale asked, and

it was Quinn who told him about Stem and how he had given his life for Rose and the others . . . how Stem had been the one to help Jessie find her children again, even after his death.

"Never did know why everyone called him Stem," Jessie said softly. "But his mama, she named him Justice, and I recall Preacher tellin' him once that was a fine name and that his mama surely knew what she was doin' namin' him like that."

I walked with Jessie and her children down to her own cabin, and it was as we were walking that it suddenly hit me that soon enough Jessie would be leaving . . . that she wouldn't be with us on the ranch anymore . . . that, worst of all, I wouldn't have her anymore.

"Oh, I don't think I'm going to be able to bear it when you leave here, Jessie," I said, a part of me knowing it was selfish to say, but I couldn't help it. "It would be like losing a part of my heart, and I don't think I have much more I can afford to lose."

Jessie chuckled her dry, comforting kind of chuckle and hugged me close to her. "Well now, honey, that's the thing about hearts," she said as she patted my back. "They tend to mend in spite o' our doubts, and Lord, we been given some doubts, ain't we? But they do mend, mebbe not the same as before. But I kindly like t' imagine them little mendin' scars bein' like new roads for us t' follow . . .

"And who's to say you can't come callin' down that new road of mine, huh?" she added with a sweet smile on her old face.

When she finally pulled away, I had the strangest feeling . . . almost like that day when Quinn and I had stood on the porch of our cabin and felt that new wind blow into our lives . . . And I knew then that it had blown into Jessie's life as well.

December 5, 1873 . . . .

The snow has started to fall again this morning: big flakes that blow and swirl past the windows, already piling on top of what was left before. I think the mighty hand of Providence held it back just until Jessie's family made it safe to the ranch. And being that he did, Quinn and Jack now have all the help they could ask for.

Medicine Weasel and One Shot are teasing John-Charles in Blackfoot somewhere outside. I can hear them all laughing as I hold Mara Lee and try to write this at the same time. But I feel led to write this . . . to say it seems as if the pieces to the puzzle of all of are lives are coming together now more than ever before.

Medicine Weasel made a rare appearance at the cabin this evening while the men were down at the barn, checking on one of the horses that was getting ready to foal. Rose and Patrick had taken off earlier with Gale to Jack and Lillie's for a game of Drop the Handkerchief with Jessie's grandchildren, so I was left alone with Mara Lee when I heard the knock at the door. I had to call out, "Come on in!" twice before I saw the door finally open and Medicine Weasel cautiously step inside.

I could tell he had tried to make an effort with his

appearance, dressing in some of the clothes Jack had given him and braiding his long white hair, but he still looked too thin. I tried to steel myself against the memory of the proud medicine man who had saved Jack's life all those years ago.

Medicine Weasel smiled at me then sat down on the floor in front of the fireplace with a slight groan. Then he looked at me for what seemed like an eternity before he talked.

"Jessie's people, with hair like the buffalo, do they fare as well as the whites?" he asked, and when I told him no, he merely nodded, as if he suspected as much. He pulled out a piece of jerky and chewed off a tiny bit and stared into the fire.

"So, getting land of their own, this has been a difficult thing?" he asked finally.

"Yes," I said. "There are some whites that don't want them to have any land. But they didn't put their faith in those people; they put their faith in God."

"And it has turned out well for them. This is good news," he said, rising to leave. Then he stopped at the door as if a thought had suddenly occurred to him. "You were right," he said. "Grandfather does bring you hope to fill where those dead pieces used to be."

December 6, 1873 . . .

Another day of snow; falling like big feathers through the gray sky, hitting the earth with a hush that seems almost impossible. I can just barely make out Medicine Weasel's lodge from the window, but I do see the spirals of smoke trailing upward before they're swept back down with the snow. The valley and beyond looks like it's been covered by a huge white blanket, and I feel like going back to bed for some reason.

I think Mara Lee feels the same; I can hear the soft baby chatter she does when she's drifting off to sleep. She said her first word today, which sounded to me like, "Nodunt," and it wasn't until I had her repeat it in front of Quinn that Rose and Patrick looked at each other and burst into a round of laughter.

"Bird's saying, 'No, don't,' Mama," Patrick said, and Quinn and I laughed as he picked up Mara Lee and brushed over her thick, black curls. I should have known. "No, don't" has become the most-said words around this cabin since she's started crawling and reaching for things.

Well, I best lay this pen down and get to work while our little Bird takes a nap—in spite of me wanting to join her.

Later—

I have an idea now why I had such a yearning to take a nap earlier.

I'd just finished another round of mending and then washing and stringing clothes all over the cabin until they started taking on the appearance of oversized Christmas ornaments, draped on everything as they were, when Rose and Patrick came in with a fresh load of wood to tell me they had invited everyone over for a Bible story.

I was almost tempted to run to Medicine Weasel and One Shot's lodge and stay there, but there was such a happy look to their eyes that I didn't have the heart to really run . . . or to say no.

Quinn knew it, too, for there was a sympathetic smile

on his tired face as he quickly set the children into action helping him straighten up the cabin before our company arrived. And truth is, I'm so glad I didn't say no . . .

We watched them from the porch as they came from all directions, trudging through the snow, hanging on to the ropes that connected us all to each other. And as I stood there, I thought how blessed we were to have such a family that would go through a bitterly cold night to get together . . . and to hear God's Word.

Jessie, her two girls, and Lillie quickly herded the little ones in and got them settled, then set to fixing some coffee to go with the rice puffs Lillie had made special. Medicine Weasel and One Shot surprised us by coming in, too. And after they had convinced us they were more comfortable sitting on the floor with the children, choosing which story to read was the next order of business. Everyone finally settled on Moses and the burning bush.

And that's when the questions began: "Well, how come people always have to take their shoes off when an angel comes? Are their shoes real dirty?" said one. "I'll bet the angels just don't like shoes. They don't need them anyways, 'cause they fly," said another. "No, that was the angel of the Lord—that means God," said another, followed by a great sigh. "But he's God. He don't need shoes, either," said one. "I wish we didn't," whispered yet another.

It was all I could do not to laugh, so I tried my best to keep my eyes off of Jessie, Lillie, and the others, who I knew were having a time of it by the way they were excusing themselves to disappear into the kitchen every so often. I went on, telling how Moses asked God if he could see him face to face, and that's when Jessie's grandbaby Noel leaned forward, his dark eyes wide with the thought of it.

"Miss Callie, is God black?" he blurted out suddenly, and I felt every small head in the room look up to study my face. Even Medicine Weasel appeared to be extremely interested in my answer as he leaned forward, too, waiting.

"I don't think God is a *color* at all," Gale said, suddenly speaking up before I could. "He can't be. Because the Bible says he's perfect love, and there isn't a color to *love*."

Noel sat back, satisfied, and Medicine Weasel did, too, as if the weight of the world were suddenly lifted off their shoulders. Gale turned and looked at me then, his eyes searching my face.

"Am I right?" he asked finally.

"Yes, you surely are," I said, smiling. And this time, I did look up to Jessie and Lillie and the others, and when our eyes met, it was with the feeling of wonder over this young boy who seemed to have wisdom far beyond his years. When I glanced over at Rose, I could see she was looking at him in a different light as well.

"You're pretty smart when you want to be, Gale," she admitted, and Gale grinned, looking suddenly like he'd won a prize.

I do thank you, Lord, for this night. For showing me that some great blessings can come in the smallest of packages . . . and for giving me the chance to learn that those packages can be delivered at any time.

But especially when we least expect them.

The Other Side of Jordan

Where have the days gone?

It's been snowing here the past few days like it has no plans to stop, and we have all had to pitch in, trying in any way we can to keep ahead of the snow, riding through thick drifts to spread out as much hay as we can for the cattle. Jessie, Lillie, all of us are pitching in—even Medicine Weasel and One Shot, although neither of them has much use for cattle. *Buffalo*, now, they know enough to dig through to the grass, One Shot explained.

It's been like this: up before sunrise, cook, clean, kiss the baby and hand her to Rose, then ride out as fast as I can, praying that somehow I don't run into a deep ravine or an outcropping of rock that has been hidden by the snow and also praying that I don't lose the bundle of hay, that I'll find enough cattle to give the hay to . . . that no one comes up lost or frostbit . . .

Yet every time we ride back in at the end of the day, I see the strong spirit of endurance among us that wasn't there before. I see our family pulling together for all they're worth because now it's not just another day. Somewhere along the way, God has sealed it in our hearts that it is our *future* we're working toward . . . our land.

Quinn said as much tonight when we finally made it into the cabin, so tired and dirty.

"Did you see everyone out there today? Did you ever think it would feel so good to feel so tired?" he said, smiling down at me like we had just come in from a dance, not a blizzard, as I took off my bonnet.

I looked up at him then, and I knew by the look in his

eyes that my hair was sticking up every which way to Sunday.

"No, I didn't," I said, trying to keep my face straight, and then we couldn't keep ourselves from laughing. Once our laughter had died down, Quinn took me in his strong arms and hugged me to him. "The joy of the Lord *is* our strength, isn't it, lass?" he said, his voice thick with emotion and thankfulness . . . and I couldn't help but agree.

It has finally stopped snowing. I can almost hear the valley sigh along with my loved ones who are sleeping now . . . and I have just spotted a huge bull elk looking through the window at me, so close his nose blows circles of steam against the glass. Five years ago such a sight would have scared me to pieces. Five years ago a lot of things would have scared me to pieces.

I wonder if he will leave if I stand up. I have the oddest urge to go and put my hands against the glass where those circles of steam are . . .

December 11, 1873 . . .

It's so bitterly cold out there that everyone stays inside today, feeding the fireplace wood like you might feed a starving friend. Rose is working on her sampler, much to my surprise, and Patrick is carving away at something, but neither one is talking much.

Between Mercy's birthday and Christmas coming up, everyone has become so secretive around here, you can't get a simple answer to a question.

I just asked Quinn if my old washtub might be down at the barn, and he looked up from putting more wood on the fire, startled. "And why would you be lookin' down there, lass?" he said. Rose and Patrick looked at each other and grinned.

Mara Lee, not wanting to be left out, yelled, "Nodunt!" from her crib, causing us all to laugh.

December 14, 1873 . . .

So much work to do today and still so bitter cold out . . .

I wonder what *is* down in that barn.

December 15, 1873 . . .

It's Mercy's *fourth* birthday today. Sometimes it seems like only yesterday that I was holding her in my arms for the very first time. Then there are times when I look at her and imagine her being so much older than the little body that holds all she is.

Today she was just a little girl, though, smiling shyly as everyone gathered at Jack and Lillie's to celebrate. Preacher and Willa were the first to show up after all of us, braving the winding, snow-choked trail to get to Mercy, and Peach wasn't far behind them in coming. Even Medicine Weasel and One Shot seemed determined to witness Mercy's big day. Looking around at all of their faces, it wasn't hard to figure out why. Mercy, as was her way, had awed them by her heart . . . awed all of us, even as young as she was.

But it was Jack who seemed almost moved to tears as he watched his little girl opening her gifts, patting her small head that had been bound with the bright new kerchief Lillie had made special for her birthday.

"Pa said it was an angel that came the day she was born," John-Charles said, seeming to sense Jack's feelings. "He said it was because God wanted the world to have Mercy in it."

We all fell silent for a moment, his words meaning more than he really knew to this ragtag group of settlers who have prayed for mercy too many times to count in our lives. It was Preacher who finally broke the silence, his face telling of his own struggles.

"Well, your pa couldn't have been more right," Preacher said, looking at all of us.

"I *know* it was an angel unaware, Uncle Jack," Patrick said with a conviction that hadn't left him after all this time. "I didn't get to see that one. But I'm always on the lookout now, just in case."

Mercy, who had been gingerly picking up each gift that had been made for her, looked up, then chanced a quick glance over Peach's way. "But angels have their own teeth, right?" she said, and delighted laughter broke out all over the room as the little ones surrounded her, oohing and ahhing over her presents.

"Looks like you're going to go down in history 'bout them teeth, Peach," Jessie said with a teasing look in her eyes as we moved toward the kitchen and let the little ones play. Peach, who had been looking quite sentimental himself, turned and winked at Jessie's children.

"Ya never know, old woman," he said with a kindly look to his eyes. "I might jes surprise ya and do somethin' real rash."

"Well, if selling land to colored folk ain't rash, I don't

know what is," Jessie said, enjoying their banter, and it was easy to see Peach did, too. He chuckled but looked real pleased with himself.

"Maybe what he means by *rash* is proposing to Widow Spence," Lillie said, grinning, and Peach blushed so hard it made us all laugh again.

"Speakin' of weddings," Quinn said, glancing Preacher and Willa's way. "It keeps snowin' like this, Preacher, and we're going to have a time of it gettin' the lumber in to start raisin' your church."

"What say ya?" Peach said then, his attention suddenly piqued. We explained to him about the plans for the church—and how Preacher and Willa would marry as soon as it was finished, all of us talking more excitedly as we went on. To have a real church in town instead of a tent seemed to make it feel more permanent. But especially to Willa.

"Once it's finished, we'll marry," Willa added with a curve to her lips that was the starting of a smile.

"Oh, we'll have our church built by spring, Willa," Preacher said with a determined look. "Count on it." Then he grinned. "It's easier getting a fishhook in than it is taking it out—but you should know that after all these years."

We all had a good laugh then—even Willa, who tried her best to appear mortified, but we could tell she was secretly pleased, too . . .

It *would* be wonderful to have a real church. The more roots a tree can put down, the better chance it has to stand against a storm when it blows in, my pa always used to say. I have a feeling that's what we've all been doing lately, without maybe even realizing it. Putting down roots.

I told Mercy tonight as we were leaving that many

birthdays from now she would be walking down the aisle of our church with her husband and she would remember this night when she was four and our church was just a dream.

Mercy nodded somberly and looked up at me with those huge green eyes of hers, clutching the new rag doll Jessie had made for her in her arms. She crooked her finger for me to bend down. "I'll remember, Aunt Callie," she whispered, and cocked her head to look me in the eyes for a long moment. Then she smiled, and the words she whispered next, I don't think I'm likely to forget.

"You're not scared anymore, are you . . . "

It is snowing *again*.

December 21, 1873 . . .

Sabbath. The last few days of snow made it impossible for us to get to town to hear Preacher today. But maybe it was just God's way of getting us to slow down, to be still and once again draw closer to him after these last days of battling once again to keep our cattle fed . . . his way of encouraging us that no matter where we are, he is with us.

As Quinn slowly opened our Bible to the Book of Isaiah, I realized that God didn't just whisper in Preacher's ear, but in my husband's ear, too, and when he began to read, I saw Jessie and her children all begin to smile and nod, saw the look of tiredness on Jack's face begin to ease: "'Remember ye not the former things, neither consider the things of old. Behold, I will do a new thing; now it shall spring forth; shall ye not know it? I will even make a way in the wilderness, and rivers in the desert.'"

It was Gale who seemed to speak for all of us, though, as he suddenly glanced up, a sweet smile on his face as if something had just occurred to him. "He *is* doing a new thing in us all, isn't he?" He looked around the room at us. "Because none of our lives are really the same as before, are they?"

I thought of Willa then, and how God had changed in an instant the way she thought all those years . . . I thought of Lillie and how he had taken her heart beyond what she would've ever thought to reach out to someone who had caused her nothing but pain . . . and of Jessie and her children, how he had proved faithful in giving them their land . . . and of Peach, dear Peach . . . and Gale, who he had led away from such sadness and given him a real place to call home . . . and Medicine Weasel, how he had given him new hope. And then I thought of how he had given me a new hope, too.

I pondered how he *had* blown this new wind into all of our lives . . . and when I finally glanced over at Quinn, smiling down at Rose and Patrick with such love, I realized it didn't even have to be Christmas to know that we had all been given a gift better than what we could ever imagine . . .

December 22, 1873 . . .

Christmas is in the air around here. Everyone is tiptoeing around, casting furtive little glances each other's way, then smiling like the cat that ate the canary . . .

I was just down at the barn, looking for that little

washtub so we could fill it with a spiced ginger drink I want to make for Christmas Day, when Jasper and Honey—even their pups—kept watching after me as if I was on the verge of breaking a commandment. They made me feel so guilty I finally came back in here to get warm again. I honestly haven't been snooping.

And I never found my washtub, either.

Quinn brought in a fine tree tonight, and we had such a good time of it, trimming it with strings of popcorn and red berries and walnuts wrapped in little bits of tinfoil. We just couldn't spare the candles to add to the trimmings, but the children don't seem to mind.

Rose and Patrick are sitting by the fireplace now, as I write this, looking at the tree with pleased little looks on their faces. But Mara Lee, who can't bear being that far from the "pretty," crawls over to the tree and lies just beneath the bottom branches, looking up with those eyes of hers, wide as saucers. She knows she isn't to touch, so she holds her chubby fingers out, just a whisper away from the branches. *So close*, her expression says, *so close, but so far* . . .

December 23, 1873 . . .

Overcast, windy day today and so cold that even the logs of this cabin creak and groan their protest.

It's a good day to finish up my own little surprises for everyone, little journal. I have just a few more stitches to make on the shirt I made for Quinn. Patrick's new trousers and Rose's dress are ready, as well as the sweet little burlap dolls I made for Rose, Mercy, and Mara Lee. Quinn showed me the three little wooden "treasure boxes" he made for Patrick, John-Charles, Gale, and Jessie's grandbaby, Noel, and I only hope Rose doesn't feel left out, thinking of herself as one of the boys like she does . . .

Mara Lee is leaning out of her crib for all she is worth, trying to reach the tree—I best close for now before our little Bird falls out on her head . . .

Early Christmas Eve morning, and not a mouse stirs . . . but a little Bird does, and as I look down at her sleeping in my arms, I want to thank you, Lord, for all you have given me . . . and for sending your Son to bring light into this sometimes dark, lonely world. I can't imagine any mother or father not understanding what a great sacrifice that was . . .

December 25, 1873 . . .

Christmas Day. And what a beautiful day it has been. I am going to try my best to put everything down just as it happened, for I never want to forget this day. I recall Mama saying that life isn't measured by the breaths we take . . . but by the times that take our breath away. And this day, little journal, was one of those breathtaking times.

Jack and Lillie were the first to arrive, then Gale, looking a bit shy but expectant, too, like he was hoping to see something he had only dreamed of before. Jessie and her children and grandchildren were next, with Peach, Medicine

Weasel, and One Shot following close behind. But it was Preacher and Willa's entrance that gave us such a surprise, for they had brought Mr. Audrey and the twins with them!

"I hope you don't mind, Callie," Willa said, taking me off to one side as we watched our men greeting a slightly dazed-looking Mr. Audrey. "But when we went by to check on them, Percy broke down to Shawn, saying Leah seems to have gone for good, and all I could think of was that poor man and those girls being alone on Christmas."

We watched Rose and Mercy take the twins' hands and lead them up to the loft, chattering happily . . . but I couldn't help noticing how thin and drawn the girls looked, their pretty blonde hair usually so well kept like their mama's. Today they looked frowzied, like they had just woke up.

"Mind?" I said, smiling grimly. "Shame on me for not thinking of it myself." Lillie and Jessie had joined us by then, and they looked about the same as I felt. So we did the only thing we knew to do, and that was to try and make it as good a Christmas for them as we could.

As soon as the men headed for the barn to look after the horses, Jessie's girls, who are as tender-hearted as their mama, joined us as we moved the table in front of the fireplace, taking extra special care to set it quick with extra plates so they would feel they had been expected all along. I got out my best tablecloth, and Jessie and her girls went and fetched some pine snippings that Willa thought might look "festive" placed around the bowls and platters of food we had made. Then Lillie ran to her cabin and brought back two real pretty silver candleholders that, she told us with a chuckle, she'd won in a card game in Virginia City years ago.

"I always wondered why I carried them with me. Wondered what I would do with them out here," she said, shaking her pretty head. "Now I know they were meant for this day—to cheer Mr. Audrey and his girls."

Rose came down not long after that and took me to one side to tell me she thought it would be a good thing if I gave her presents to the Audrey twins. "I don't mean to hurt your feelings, Mama," she said, solemn as a judge. "But I just figured they might get cheered up if they thought someone remembered them today . . . with their mama forgettin' and all." Mercy, who was standing behind her, nodded her agreement, then smiled.

I hugged my sweet little girl then and looked over at Willa and the rest of the women and saw we were all trying to blink back our tears.

Gale was next, bringing out a beautiful wooden cross carved with vines and flowers from behind his back. "Miss Callie, I carved this for you," he said, suddenly looking torn as to how to say what he needed to say. "I thought if you didn't mind, I would give it to Mr. Audrey. I remember you saying to keep our eyes fixed on the cross when we're troubled, and I thought maybe it might help him to have something to look at."

Patrick and John-Charles were so desperate by then to think of something to give they were offering their presents as well, but we told them the dolls were enough.

"I never seen a family like this in all my life," Willa said. "Too bad we're out in the middle of nowhere; the world could use a good dose of you all."

By the time the men hit the porch, stomping the snow from their shoes, we had the presents set out, the table ready, the candles lit . . . and a baby wild from trying to get out of her crib to reach all the "pretties."

"Mine!" Mara Lee yelled, clear as a bell, shocking us all

before we burst out laughing. "That's our Bird," Patrick said, real proud, as he rubbed his hand over her curls.

But it was Mr. Audrey's astonished face that said it all as he looked in wonder at the spread before him. We had him and the girls open their gifts then, and I saw great tears come to his eyes as he pulled the brown paper off the cross Gale had so lovingly carved. The girls smiled sweet smiles, showing him the burlap dolls, then thanked us in such a grateful way, you would have thought they had been given a china doll like the ones in their mercantile. Rose and Mercy looked at each other, pleased as anything.

After Mr. Audrey hugged his girls, he turned and faced us again.

"First I thought we would be alone today," he started, then cleared his throat. "Then when Preacher and Miss Willa came by, I told myself that it would be good for the girls. But it's been real good for me, too, and I thank God for all of you today, for making us feel like part of your family."

"Be careful, Percy. They're real sneaky like that," Willa said then, trying to make him smile. "Look at me; I was happy living alone and being an independent divorcée who didn't believe in God. I start coming around this bunch, and the next thing you know I'm engaged—to a preacher!" We all laughed at that—even Percy.

Preacher just shook his head as we were seated and said wryly, "I can't imagine a better time to begin a prayer."

Such a good prayer it was, too. I don't think I'll ever forget the laughter around our table or the love. Or the way Percy and his girls looked as they finally waved their good-byes to us. Medicine Weasel explained it best as he stood next to me and Quinn on the porch and watched them go.

"Grandfather is giving him new pieces now, to replace the ones he lost," he said, then he turned from us and, without another word, shuffled slowly back to his little lodge in the snow.

Rose and Patrick were so excited from the day that we could hardly get them to sleep tonight. Rose had to tell me how glad she was that Mercy liked the sampler she had done for her—the one that made all of us laugh so hard, our stomachs hurt: "Better love hath no woman," it read, "than to cut off her hair for a friend." Patrick opened and shut his treasure box so many times, I thought the lid would come off. Then he said something that nearly brought both Quinn and me to tears.

We were tucking him in, and just as I got the blanket under his chin, he looked up at me, his eyes wide in the dark. "Mama," he said, "did Mary kiss baby Jesus when he was born?" and when I told him yes, he nodded and then seemed to think of something else.

"I wonder if she knew she was kissing God when she did that," he said, his voice trailing off sleepily, and Quinn and I just looked at each other in wonder.

"Just when I think I know their minds . . . ," Quinn said, grinning.

Once we were downstairs again, Quinn gave me the surprise he had been hiding away all this time. Well, actually it was from him *and* Jessie. Quinn had made a beautiful frame, carved with vines and curlicues, to hold a sweet memory quilt Jessie had made me, much like the ones she and Lillie had made for themselves, each scrap taken from a piece of my life. Jessie had sewn the memories together, I thought, looking at the tiny, intricate stitches, like a quilt of words.

I gave Quinn the shirt I'd made him, and he went on and on about it, like it was the best he ever had. Then we grinned at each other and hugged, sitting in front of the fireplace with our heads together like two little kids.

"I wish Mr. Audrey had what we do, Quinn," I said after a while, for some reason the memory of Percy's sweet face coming before me. Quinn turned and looked at me then, and I saw he had been thinking of Percy, too.

"I do, too, lass," he said. "I wish it for him *and* for his girls."

As I sit here writing this, I can't help wondering what could ever possess a mother to leave her children like that. Quinn says that's why she could leave, because she *wasn't* a mother, but I have this niggling suspicion there's more to it than that . . .

Funny, those words of Jessie's from that dream I had keep coming back to me as I write this: "Pray, and the good Lord will do the rest. He always does . . ."

I do pray for that poor family . . . and for Leah Audrey, too. I wonder where she is on a night when being with family seems to matter so much.

December 29, 1873 . . .

Willa came tonight to deliver some news, and my mind just refuses to believe it. She said Mrs. Audrey is on her way to Missouri . . . to be put in *jail*. Willa said Percy came to ask her if she would watch the girls while he went to see what happened, and she told him she would. It seems he got the news from a man that had come into the mercantile saying he'd been to Virginia City and had seen an old woman pointing out Mrs. Audrey on the street. The man said she had been standing just a hair's distance from him. He said he saw the marshal's men come right for her and waste no time in apprehending her—and that she had begged him to tell her husband what had happened and that they were taking her back to Missouri. The man didn't know much more than that . . .

Even if there was more, I don't think I could write it. Now that Willa is gone, the only thing I can think to do is pray for them all while I wait for Quinn to come back from checking on the cattle.

I feel like that strange dream I had has come true . . . Only it's not a dream. It's a nightmare . . . especially for poor Percy and his girls.

And Mrs. Audrey . . . Is she scared? Is she looking out at the cold night sky tonight, thinking of her husband, of her little girls?

I can't help but wonder.

December 30, 1873 . . .

The sky is such a vivid blue this morning, the mountains rising up so sharp and clear in the distance, that I feel like we've woke up in another place. But the pitiful bawling of the cattle tells me we haven't.

Quinn just left to go check on them with Patrick and Gale trailing behind him while Jack and John-Charles tend the horses. Rose will be in soon from milking Tulip, and I plan to put her straight to work helping me get the bread started—and anything else I can think of to keep her busy.

"Our Rose finds out about Mrs. Audrey, and there will be no end to it," Quinn said just before he left, the look on his face somewhere between a grin and a grimace, and I know he is right.

He was also right when he said we all need to stand in prayer for *all* the Audreys. Good or bad, he said, we're a community now, a church family, and we have to stick by each other in times of trouble.

We gathered at our cabin tonight to pray for the Audreys, Quinn being the one to go round up the troops after the work was finished. As I watched them all file into our cabin behind Quinn, I couldn't help feeling so blessed to have a husband like him, so willing to do what he felt the Lord expected of him.

Before we started praying, though, he sat Rose down with the other children and explained to them what had happened. And just as he predicted, no sooner was the sad story out of his mouth than a spark of "I told you so" lit up Rose's eyes.

"Now, Rosie," Quinn said in a gentle but firm voice, "we don't know the full reason of it yet, and what we are here to do tonight is pray for *all* of them. Do you understand?"

Rose nodded silently, her love for her pa outweighing her urge to crow. Quinn recognized the urge, though, and I saw him steel himself against smiling. Then he turned to the rest of the children, who were watching him and Rose with wide, serious eyes. Jessie, Lillie, and I looked at each other and smiled.

"I want you all to listen to the Lord's Word I'm about to read. And maybe you'll understand better what God says we are supposed to do," he said. Then he sat down next to me, bowing his large frame over the Bible in his work-worn hands as he slowly turned the pages.

"I came across this scripture this morning in First Corinthians, and I thought it fitting," Quinn said, looking up from the Bible to all of us in the room. Everyone nodded quietly, and he began to read: "'And those members of the body, which we think to be less honourable, upon these we bestow more abundant honour; and our uncomely parts have more abundant comeliness. For our comely parts have no need,'" Quinn read softly. "'But God hath tempered the body together, having given more abundant honour to that part which lacked. That there may be no schism in the body; but that the members should have the same care one for another.'" Quinn looked up, and I saw Jessie's eyes meet with his. She smiled, finishing the scripture for him:

"'And whether one member suffer, all the members suffer with it,'" Jessie recited, tears in her eyes but her face aglow with the soft smile of a woman who had lived by those very words. Then she looked at her children. "'Or one member be honoured, all the members rejoice with it.'"

Jessie's daughters, Sara and Rachel, were dabbing their eyes with their handkerchiefs. Even their husbands were blinking hard, but Jessie's son, Jonah, allowed his tears to run free down his face as he smiled at us all.

"And that's why they call him, 'the First and the Last,'

'cause there ain't *never* gonna be another talk such as that," Jonah said with deep sincerity.

Jack cleared his throat, and I saw him glance over to John-Charles, then to Medicine Weasel, and he said, "And there ain't no one better than him that listens, either."

We joined hands then, and as we did, I felt as if we were knitted together by more than just our hands but by our spirits, too; each of us *had* been where the Audreys were now, maybe not in the same way . . . but we all knew what it was like to suffer. And we all knew how good it felt to know God was holding our hand through that suffering in the form of another person who believed.

Quinn began the prayer, each of us adding to it as we felt led, when suddenly I heard Rose's small voice saying, "And, dear Lord, forgive me for my mean thoughts. I don't know if Mrs. Audrey really is the fearless Banditti of the Plains, but whatever she's done mean, well, I've done mean, too. So I'm asking you to help her like you've helped me and just about everyone else here, too."

Quinn and I smiled at each other, and we all said amen. When I looked up I saw Gale was smiling at Rose, too, like he couldn't believe she could surprise him again. Patrick saw the look and nodded like he understood.

"She's pretty smart, Gale," he said with all of the well-earned wisdom of a brother who has endured. Then he added, " . . . when she wants to be."

December 31, 1873 . . .

Another cold but sunny day. Could it be God's way of telling us we are on the verge of a bright New Year? I would like to think so.

It seems so much has happened since I started this little journal, and it hasn't yet been a full year. When I think on it, we've come so far in such a short time—more than I could have imagined, and I have a pretty healthy imagination. We *have* seen some bad times, but we've also seen so much good. Most of all, we've learned more about holding on to our faith and about seeing with our own eyes the promise of God's hand move because of it.

This afternoon, while I was watching Mara Lee sleeping, I started thinking about all the times when I was just a young girl imagining what it would be like to be a mother and a wife. It got me to thinking so much that I went and pulled out my old journal—the first one I ever kept. And as I was thumbing through the pages, I came to an entry I had wrote just before we had left our farm in Missouri to set out on that wagon train for California. "With age comes wisdom and virtue," I read. And I admit I had to chuckle.

What eighteen-year-old girl knows of such things? I guess back then I thought I already had life figured out . . .

You know what I think now, little journal?

What a blessing it was that I didn't . . .

January 1, 1874 . . .

I woke up this morning to my husband and children standing over the bed with the biggest grins on their faces.

"Say it, Bird," Patrick said suddenly, looking over at Mara Lee, who was planted happily in Quinn's arms. She looked from Patrick to Rose to Quinn, then finally she looked at me and grinned, too.

"Mah-mah!" she said just as plain as if she had been

saying it forever. We all laughed as I struggled to sit up in the bed. Then it hit me that it was still much too early for them all to be up—either that, or I had overslept for the first time in my life. I started to throw the covers back then, but Quinn stopped me.

"Mara Lee was just the beginning of your surprise. We didn't even plan that part," he said happily, looking to Rose and Patrick.

"We already made you breakfast, Mama," Rose blurted out, unable to contain herself. "And then you get to do any old thing you feel like. And not chores, either. Pa says this is *your* day to play."

"You can even use my treasure box if you want to, Mama," Patrick offered in a gesture of extreme sacrifice.

"We just wanted to say we love you, Callie," Quinn said, and Mara Lee clapped and said, "Mah-mah!" again.

What I did next, I think any normal mother of three children, living on a ranch out in the middle of nowhere, would do. I took one long look at my sweet, loving family and promptly burst into tears.

I have just come back in and have so much to tell. But first I want to say how grateful I am to have such a family as mine. I will never forget the looks on their faces as they sent me off for a visit to Willa's today, so happy over what they had done that you would have thought it was for them, not me.

Quinn secured the runners onto the wagon and hitched the team as Gale, happy to be a part of it, packed the front seat with hot, flat rocks covered with straw, then Rose and Patrick topped me off with a goodly amount of blankets to make sure I stayed warm, and off I went.

Never had the cold felt so good as I watched the beauty of the snowy landscape go by me: the immense trees bowing low with ice and snow that sparkled in the sun . . . the way the valley rolled and swelled white all the way up to the mountains, no other sound but the steady drum of the horses' hooves as we wound around the long trail that led out of the valley. And the more I rode along, the more I got to thinking I needed to go see Peach instead of Willa.

To say God was with me is an understatement, for I only had a vague idea of where his cabin was from listening to Jessie's children talking of it. Even now, I can't really explain it, but I just knew that was where I wanted to go.

Finally, after what seemed like hours, I came to a short clearing and spotted a small cabin a little farther up the slope in the woods with smoke trailing from the chimney. I turned the team in that direction and had only climbed halfway up the slope when I saw Peach come out on the porch with his rifle at his side.

"Are ya friend or foe?" he hollered, squinting at me.

I said, "I'm Callie!" then laughed, and I heard him chuckle, too.

"Well, that makes all the diff'rence in the world," Peach said. "Light from yer wagon and come set a spell." And so, as soon as he had turned my horses into his barn, that's just what I did. I'll say, too, I was pleasantly surprised to see that the inside of Peach's cabin wasn't what I expected it to be. First of all, it was cleaner than I ever saw a single man's cabin to be. Whether it had come from Peach's new turn of heart or had always been that way didn't seem to matter as I sat on the chair Peach pulled next to the fire for me. I glanced around the cabin and noticed that Peach's little bed was covered with the whitest sheet I'd ever seen. On the other side of the room was a sturdy rough-hewn wooden table with a single chair, but what really got my attention was the little cracked jar filled with what looked to be nearly a dozen faded paper roses.

While I rested with a cup of coffee in front of the fire, Peach set about fixing us some "vittles," and while he did, we talked small talk. Or I should say Peach talked. He told me how he'd left his home in "Virginny" after the war and had come west to look for gold, but after nearly starving to death he'd decided it was easier to find game than gold. He said that all the years of trapping ended up bringing him more money than he would ever need.

"Thing is, money don't make fer good company," he said, shaking his head. There was something about the painful look to his eyes that told me then that he had suffered more than his fair share of loneliness, and that's when I knew I had been right to follow my feelings and come.

"No, it doesn't," I said. "But friends do, if you let them."

Peach looked at me with a hopeful expression on his face. Then, after a pause long enough to take a breath, he asked me if I had heard about the Audreys. I told him yes, and he went on to tell me he'd heard about it when he went into town and "jes happened upon Widow Spence," who had heard it from Mrs. Pumphrey, who had been told by Percy himself, according to Peach.

As Peach handed me a steaming plate of his green-corn

pudding and bachelor biscuits, I caught him studying me for a long moment. Then he went over to the little makeshift cupboard in the room and took what looked to be an old, faded piece of advertisement from one of the drawers.

"Now, I ain't showed a livin' soul this-here piece until you, Miss Callie," he said gravely. "But I figger it's time someone knowed of it." He handed me the paper, and when I looked at it, I saw Mrs. Audrey's face staring back up at me underneath the large black lettering that said she was "wanted." The paper said she had done "heinous" crimes not fitting to a person of her gender and was wanted for further questioning as to the whereabouts of a gentleman who was last seen in her company. After I got over my shock, I asked him where he had got it, and he told me he had come across it by way of an old half-crazy woman who sold paper roses on the streets of Virginia City. He said he always tried to buy a rose from her when he went to town but that the last time she had sold him his rose, she told him she wanted to show him a picture of her "daughter." She had opened up the piece of paper I now held and laughed a crazy laugh. "She ain't really my daughter," she'd said. "But she could've been." He said he had to buy nearly her whole lot of paper roses to get the wanted poster from her. Then he worried after he got home that she might have had other copies of it anyway.

"Leah Audrey was mostly mean as a snake, as fer as I kin recall," he said then. "But I figgered that man of hers was good and them little ones shouldn't have to pay for what she'd done. I never knowed my own ma, her dyin' right after I was born . . . but I always kindly imagined that I would've liked t' have knowed her . . ."

He had such a wistful look about his craggy face that I wanted to rush over and hug him. But knowing Peach, I resisted . . . for another moment or so. Then, unable to bear it, I did rush over and hug him. He looked startled at first, then he looked pleased as anything, a bright grin spreading across his face to show his fine, white teeth.

"Why, Miss Callie, I believe that's about the best thing that's happened t' me in a long time," he said. "That feller of your'n said I didn't know what I was missin', but now I think I do."

We both laughed again, but soon afterward we noticed the sun on its way down, and I was forced to leave the warmth of the little cabin to make my way back home. Peach hitched the team for me then said he would escort me most of the way back, being that I "was a lady and all." We rode in silence almost the entire way home, until we reached the head of the trail that led into our valley. Then I saw Peach pull back on his horse and look back at me as he waited for me to catch up.

"Ya know what's funny?" he said, when I finally reached him. "I was jes wishing earlier t'day that I could have me some comp'ny. And here you showed up at my door . . . How's that for a wish comin' true?"

"Did you ever think God might have heard you wishing?" I said, suddenly realizing my urge to go to Peach had been just that. "Sometimes a wish can sound just like a prayer if Someone's listening just right."

Peach looked at me real thoughtful-like, then he smiled, and I couldn't help but smile back.

"No, I never did consider such a thing," he said finally as he turned his horse away to leave. "But I might jes have t' think on that tonight, Miss Callie. I might jes have t' think on it."

I watched him ride away until he was long out of sight, and as I did, I couldn't help thinking how looking at Peach, you would never know the heart that lay inside him. How a man that most wouldn't give the time of day to had took it upon himself to try to protect a wanted woman for the sake of her husband and two little girls . . . Then I looked down at the faded poster Peach had given me, and I realized something.

I realized what the Good Book meant about being as wise as a serpent but as gentle as a dove, because people can fool you. And sometimes that's a good thing, to find out you were wrong. But there were times, too, that it was bad.

Percy Audrey was on my mind through the rest of the evening, but I waited until after the children's bedtime to show the rest of the family the wanted poster Peach had given me. The first thing Quinn said was, "Next time you decide to go on a spur-of-the-moment adventure, can you at least let me know where you're off to?"

"Well now, Quinn, how would that be spur of the moment then?" Jack said, winking at me. Then he motioned to the loft above where Rose and Patrick were sleeping. "Apple never does fall too far from the tree, does it, sis?" and everyone had a good laugh at that.

But then, as the paper got passed from hand to hand and I began to tell them all that Peach had said, the room got quiet, and I sensed everyone was wondering what would become of Percy and the twins.

"Why, Jack, you know who Peach was talking about?" Lillie said, looking up after a while. "It was Alder Rose. I used to watch her from the window of my room as she walked the streets. I haven't thought of that poor woman in such a long time." Lillie shook her head, then she turned to look at me. "How strange is it that Mrs. Audrey would end up being caught by the words of a crazy woman no one ever paid much attention to?"

"Well, the Bible says the Lord will use the foolish things to confound the wise," Jessie said slowly. "An' I've lived long enough to quit tryin' to figure out his ways of things because they's always turned out better'n mine in the end."

Medicine Weasel, who had been quiet up to that point, spoke up, surprising us all. All but Jack, that is.

"What was it you told me about falling on your back, Jack Wade?" he asked with a thoughtful look to his face, and I saw a light come into Jack's eyes as he smiled at his old friend.

"I said that sometimes when you're knocked flat on your back, you don't have no other choice than to look up," Jack said, looking around the room. "Maybe that's what God's doing with Leah Audrey. Maybe he's lettin' this happen now so she'll look up again."

"It's not a bad view," Medicine Weasel replied casually, then he glanced my way with a smile. "Once you decide to open your eyes to look."

We prayed again for the Audreys not long after that, all of us agreeing it was the right thing to do, no matter what

Mrs. Audrey had been accused of. Then we talked until long into the night about our own lives and how it amazed us all, looking back, to see God's hand at work in us all along the way. And now that I'm sitting here, pen in hand, I can't help wonder at the way this day turned out . . . All from me getting the simple urge to go see Peach instead of Willa.

Only something tells me now, that urge wasn't so simple.

January 2, 1874 . . .

We had a warm Chinook wind blow in overnight, but like Jack likes to say, she's a fickle lady, and she proved him right, changing her mind on me shortly after I hung the clothes out to dry. I had only been back in the cabin maybe an hour when a north wind suddenly came sweeping down the valley with no warning, freezing my laundry solid as rocks.

Willa showed up not long after I had come in with the clothes. She took one look at the shirts and trousers standing on their own by the fireplace and grinned.

"I never heard of a clothes graveyard," she said, "but I have the eeriest feeling I'm looking at one now."

"'Tis enough to spook a man, is what it is," Quinn said, grinning as he finished stoking the fire for me. Then he turned to the Audrey twins and told them the other children were down at the barn, looking over the new colt, and they scampered out. Quinn waved a quick wave to us and headed out the door, too.

"Cattle?" she said.

"Cattle," I answered, and we both laughed and sat at the kitchen table for coffee while Mara Lee napped.

I admit I didn't waste much time before I pulled out the paper with Mrs. Audrey's picture on it and showed it to her. Willa looked shocked, then grim.

"I had a feeling it was bad," she said, then sighed. "What is Percy going to *do*? How's he going to explain this to the girls?" No sooner had those words come out of Willa's mouth than we felt a cold breeze of air come through the room and turned to see Rose, Mercy, Zora, and Nora standing a short distance away, their smiles wavering as they tried to figure out what was going on. I noticed both Zora and Nora's eyes go to the paper in Willa's hands.

"My father has one of those," Zora said then. "He said it was a joke."

I saw Nora glance uncertainly at her sister then back to us. "Our mother is in trouble, isn't she?" she said, then promptly burst into tears.

Willa left with the girls not long after that, trying to comfort them as best as she could. Then I tended to our own girls. As soon as Quinn came in, we all prayed together as a family—a prayer as much for us as it was for them—and as we did, every one of us felt a peace come over us like a balm to soothe our troubled minds.

"'Tis the peace that passeth all understanding," Quinn called it before he went off to bed. And he is right, because there is so much I don't understand right now.

Like how Percy Audrey could have known that his wife was *wanted*. I just can't imagine it . . .

Lord, I won't pretend to understand what is happening because I don't. But I do know that you are with us more than ever after feeling your peace come over me tonight . . . come over us all. I just wish I could know your thoughts

... My mama used to say there was reasons for everything, and I sense there is a reason for all this to be happening, too. I pray that you show us what to do to truly be of help ... that your will be done. I always have made such a mess of things doing it my way, so I'm asking you to take my will and replace it with your own.

Because that's the only way I can see anything good coming out of this.

January 3, 1874 ...

I just woke up from a dream ... I can't recall the dream now, but there was a line of Scripture I was whispering as I opened my eyes: "The steps of a good man are ordered by the LORD: and he delighteth in his way. Though he fall, he should not be utterly cast down...."

I'm not sure what it means, but I do have the feeling right now to stand in the gap for Percy and pray. So, Lord, hear my prayer this morning and send your Holy Spirit to minister to that sweet man ... to strengthen him. And if he falls, give him a hand back up in the way that only you know how to do ...

January 7, 1874 ...

It's storming this morning. The oddest weather I've ever seen—not that I haven't ever seen a storm. But this one is different somehow. Despite the cold there's a feeling of heat in the air. Lightning is flashing in wide swipes across the sky, hovering low over the mountains as its bony fingers reach into the valley here. You can see the clouds lighting up from time to time, and it makes you crane your neck to look. It's like there's something mysterious going on just beyond what you can see.

Medicine Weasel and One Shot are watching it, standing just outside their lodge . . . I see Gale, too, standing in the doorway of the bunkhouse, looking up in awe.

It reminds me of something I heard one time, that whenever we see a storm flashing in the sky, that is when the angels are doing battle for us.

January 25, 1874 . . .

Our Sabbath, and if ever there was a group in need of hearing God speak to us and uplift our weary spirits today, it was us.

Preacher knew it, too, for he had seen the way the last couple of weeks of never-ending rain had sapped all our strength. Just before his sermon, I told him what I had thought that first day, when the lightning had come like it did, and he looked at me for a long moment then said, "Remember, Callie: Sometimes the battle is short, and sometimes it's long—or longer than what we'd like it to be. But the one thing I've noticed is, the longer the battle, the more of God's amazing work is revealed when we come out on the other side."

I thought about that, too, as I took my seat with the others and watched as Preacher made his walk to the front of the tent. Once he was situated, he looked up and smiled at us, then he leaned forward on his podium and clasped his hands together (lions' paws, Stem always called them), making us feel like he was getting ready to share some secret we had never heard before.

"I'm just wondering," he said slowly as he looked around the room. "Is there anyone else here but me who would like to see a little sunshine in their lives?"

"Did Noah?" an old miner yelled from the back, and everyone chuckled at that, even Preacher.

"Why, yes, he did. And now that you mention it, Noah had to wait fourteen days after the flood had receded before he got some good news," Preacher said as a wide grin began to spread across his face. "And here I've only made you wait until Sunday."

Everyone chuckled again, and I felt the mood starting to lift amongst us as Preacher's face grew serious with what he was setting forth to say.

"Scripture says, 'He maketh his sun to rise on the evil and on the good, and sendeth rain on the just and on the unjust.' Have you ever thought about what that means? For a long time, every time I would read that scripture I would just concentrate on the *rain* part of it, thinking it meant that God sends his *rain* down on us all." Preacher smiled. "But I was wrong.

"Because if you look at what it's really saying, it's that God is a nurturer. The world's farmer, you might say. And because he has yet to separate those who walk with him from those who don't, he won't withhold those things . . . because he wants *his* crops—his people and those who are to be his—to grow."

People were nodding all over the tent by then, and Preacher stepped away from the podium to get closer to us.

"Listen: It's going to take some sun and some rain, too, for any seed planted to struggle free from the earth. And then it's going to take a little more to keep it growing strong. It's the same with us.

"Except our sun and rain are our faith.

"That mustard seed of faith you have in your heart right now, who do you think planted it? And how do you think it's going to grow?" Preacher looked around again, studying the faces of the crowd.

"It's Jesus that is our light, our pure water. Jesus said it himself: 'If anyone is thirsty, let him come to me and drink.' The more we accept him into our lives, little by little, the more that seed is going to grow, going to take root . . .

"That mustard seed of faith," Preacher said again, a soft smile coming to his face, "is the least of all seeds; but when it is grown it is greater than the herbs and becomes a tree.

"Have any of you seen a mustard seed? The funny thing is, if you ever have, you'd never imagine the huge tree it grows into. You couldn't imagine it.

"But God could . . . God *did*.

"Folks, there is so much he has planted in you, so much he wants to see take root and grow. But there is going to be a struggle. There are going to be times when you think you'll never be able to reach hard enough or high enough to feel the warm touch of his light."

Preacher paused then, his eyes moving over our heads to the back of the tent. "But you *will* feel his light," he said finally, a look of compassion spreading across his handsome face. "And when you do, you will bloom into that tree you were always meant to be."

More than a few of us turned around then, and that's when we saw Percy Audrey standing at the back of the tent, looking like he was trying his best not to cry.

We all stayed behind in the tent after everyone else had left, knowing without really talking amongst ourselves that Percy needed our support.

As I watched Zora and Nora run to him, for a brief instant I could have sworn I saw Peach trailing out of the tent with the others, too. But the crowd started pressing forward to leave, and my attention was soon turned back to Percy, who had joined us in the front.

Percy tried his best to put on a good face. He said Leah had to stay behind in Missouri for a while to "clear up some matters." Then he tried his best to smile, but we could all see it was a great effort for him to do so. "A case of mistaken identity, I'm sure," he added, avoiding our eyes.

"They saw the paper with Mother's picture on it," Nora blurted out to him, unable to bear the war she saw going on in her pa, and that's when the mask he had tried so hard to keep on began to crack. His smile began wavering until, without warning, he broke down, crying, in front of us all. When he was finally able to be led to a chair, he sat down shakily and began to really talk.

He said he had known she was wanted before they even married, that he'd found the poster with her picture on it in Helena. "I thought if she just had a chance at a different life . . . I thought she just needed a chance," he said, looking around with a lost look on his face. "I've been so alone with this."

"You're not alone any longer, Mr. Audrey. We've been praying for you for a *long* time," Mercy said, sidling up next to him as the twins fairly clung to him on the other side. Then she took his hand in her own and patted it, and I saw Percy look down at her and smile sadly.

"I prayed, too," Percy said. "But it seemed the more I prayed, the meaner she got." He shook his head sadly.

"God hardened her heart, Mr. Audrey," Rose suddenly piped up. "Remember, he hardened Pharaoh's heart so he'd get in trouble and have to listen. I bet that's what he's done with Mrs. Audrey; he's hardened her heart, and now she's gonna have to listen."

"Rose!" I said, looking over at Quinn, who was just as shocked as I was. Patrick, Gale, and John-Charles started to edge away, sensing trouble was coming, but Preacher held his hand up.

"Now, she might have a point," he said gently. He looked at Rose, who was fairly beaming at her rescuer, and smiled before he went on. "Sometimes it takes things like this for people to come back to God—if they do at all." Preacher looked over at Percy then. "And sometimes it takes things like this for people to understand who God is—and who they are to him."

We all left for home not long after that, bundling up and climbing into our wagons for the long ride, and I can honestly say I don't think any of us said much to each other on that ride home. I think we were all thinking of what Preacher had said in his sermon about growing and about questioning whether this was part of the struggle. But most of all, I think we were thinking about what Preacher had said at the end, that sometimes it takes things like this for people to come back to God—if they do at all. And maybe we were wondering what would become of Percy and the twins when all was said and done.

I know *I* was wondering about all of it.

January 26, 1874 . . .

What a good day Rose and I have had together, one I will remember for a long time—and I hope she does, too.

It all started as we were doing yet another load of wash this morning, mainly Rose's pinafores and cambric drawers—the latter had been white only once. And that was before the first time she had put them on. Day after day of planting herself astride the top rail of the corral had permanently stained them with pine pitch, and we were having a time of it, trying to get them clean. I had said something to the effect of wondering why in the world a girl her age would spend hours perched on a rail like that, when she stopped scrubbing for a moment and gave me a thoughtful look.

"You ought to try it sometime, Mama," she said, smiling. "It's the best seat to see things in all the ranch." I don't know if it was her smile or the twinkle in her eye or remembering the sadness of Percy and his girls, but suddenly I heard myself saying, "Let's rinse these and go then. Just you and me."

"It'll be our secret?" she asked, and when I said yes, she fairly beamed. Soon we were on our way, dropping a happy Mara Lee into Jessie's arms then turning to walk arm in arm the rest of the way down to the corrals.

We took our seats, arranged our coats around us, and for a good long while we watched life go by. We laughed together over the antics of the new foal. We watched Jack and John-Charles work on a green-broke horse. Then we witnessed Quinn, Patrick, and Gale coming down a steep slope, the immense mountains framing their silhouettes as they brought a sickly cow in, puffs of snow flying up from the horses' hooves as the sound of their voices mingled in the air, and I felt like I was seeing my family for the very first time.

"You were right, Rose," I said, hugging her to me. "This *is* the best seat to see things in all of the ranch."

I feel nearly froze solid now that we're back inside. But to see the look of happiness such a simple thing like today has put into my little girl's eyes has made it well worth it.

Mara Lee is finally asleep after nearly terrorizing us at dinner tonight. Every time one of us would try to talk, she would launch into what Patrick calls her "Bird chatter," trying to outtalk us in jabbering—not to mention volume. Gale thought it was just the funniest thing. But then, Gale seems to find anything our family does fascinating. I think he's been so very alone in this world until he came here . . .

Patrick is reading the book Gale passed on to him after dinner, *Around the World in Eighty Days,* written by someone called Jules Verne. Rose is writing in her own little journal tonight, scribbling away. I just asked her how she liked Sunday school yesterday.

"Fine, Mama," she said in her cheerful little voice then went back to scribbling.

Then Quinn asked her, "What is it you're writing about, fair Rose?" and she looked up at him, great serious eyes much like his own. "I'm writin' about what's been happenin'," she said. Then she cocked her head to one side, looking between us. Finally she looked directly at me and smiled. "Every once in a while things can get real interestin' around here."

"I'm glad we can oblige you, lass," Quinn said earnestly, but after Rose nodded and went back to her writing, his eyes met mine, and I could see the laughter in them . . . and the love . . .

My cup runneth over, Lord.

January 29, 1874 . . .

Back to work again today. I've swept, dusted, and made breakfast, and now it's nearly time for lunch. Just stirred the stew. The cornbread is ready. Rose churns, singsonging to Mara Lee, "Come butter, come. Peter standing at the gate, waiting for a butter cake."

Mara Lee claps, looking so comical in the little coverall I sewed together from sugar sacks for her. She was having such a time of it with splinters constantly tormenting her knees from crawling like mad to see where everyone is going all the time that I had to do something. It seems to be working, saving both her knees and her clothes . . .

Patrick just came in with the men, took one look at Mara Lee, and laughed. "I can't wait till she gets older so I can tell her she wore gunny sacks for clothes," he said, and everyone laughed.

Everyone but Mara Lee, that is. She took one look at all of the laughing faces in the room and did something I'd never seen her do before. She puckered out her bottom lip and folded her chubby arms across her chest, refusing to look at them anymore.

Quinn says I may have saved her knees, but I've "wreaked havoc on her vanity."

The ladies of the ranch have been invited to Willa's for a little sewing get-together tomorrow. I, for one, am looking forward to it—I know the others are, too. It seems like it's been forever since we've gotten together with "just us girls" and had some normal conversation. With all that's went on lately, that will be a treat in itself.

January 31, 1874 . . .

Well, I've just come back from Willa's, and we did have a fine time of it—even if our conversation didn't end up being as normal as I had expected.

It was starting to snow a little when we were getting ready to head out, but Quinn and Jack thought quick and ran down to the river and cut some willow poles, fashioning a sort of covered wagon for us. Jessie's son, Jonah, filled the back of the wagon with some bluegrass hay, blankets, and a buffalo robe from Medicine Weasel. Then Gale volunteered to drive, so we all clambered into the back: me, Lillie, Jessie, and her two daughters, and off we went. I have to say, after we got going, I was glad for the snow, for it gave us a chance to laugh and talk the whole way over. It also gave us more of a chance to get to know Rachel and Sara better. Listening to them banter, it wasn't hard to see that the two sisters are just as sweet and funny as their mama.

By the time we reached Willa's place, we *all* felt like old friends. Willa, as always, was tickled to see company and ushered us in real quick, taking our thick shawls and scarves as she directed us to the table where the coffee and cake was waiting. Then she grinned at Gale, who was looking like a fish out of water, and told him there were books to be found on the table in her front room.

"Poor thing," Willa said, grinning. "He doesn't know it, but he's in for a long day." No sooner had she said that than there was another knock at the door, and in came Mrs. Pumphrey and Widow Spence. There was another round of greetings for Rachel and Sara, and I couldn't help thinking as we stood there, chatting to each other, that something had been mended between us all. Mrs. Pumphrey and Widow Spence, living in town as they did, had always been caught between Mrs. Audrey and the rest of us, and I saw the stress of that conflict was gone from their faces. I think Mrs. Pumphrey sensed it, too.

"It's good just to be in each other's company today, isn't it?" she said, smiling at us as she sat down with a huge sigh, and that seemed to be the sign for us all to pull our sewing from our bags.

"I guess Percy is in for a rough go of it," Mrs. Pumphrey said, as always getting right to the point. "It's almost unnatural to think of a man raising little ones on his own."

"Maybe he won't have to. Maybe those folks in Missouri will take pity on her being a mother and all," Widow Spence said shyly. She must have seen the doubt on our faces, for she ducked her head again to sew. "I just like happy endings, is all," she added softly.

Lillie and I smiled at each other, and I know it was because of the silent thought of Peach running through our minds.

"Well, the Lord works in mysterious ways, that's for sure," Jessie said, glancing to her daughters, who smiled back at her. "I never thought I'd see my babies again in my lifetime. And right here they are . . . all because of a letter . . . "

"Well, I'll be the first to say I can't imagine what will come of this mystery," Willa said. "But then, I couldn't have imagined Leah Audrey as a criminal, either. Mean maybe—but a *criminal?*" Willa shook her head.

"I never did understand why she was forever going on about that high-society family she came from," Mrs. Pumphrey said, shaking her head sadly. "I always said there were two things you didn't have to talk up: your blue blood or your faith. Because if you had a speck of either, it would show in you anyway."

"Maybe she was thinking those lies in her head was better than the truth," Lillie said then, looking around at us all with a thoughtful look on her face. "Maybe she thought if she said them enough, she would believe them as much as we did."

"I remember Jack saying once that you can run, but you just can't ever get far enough to get away from yourself," I said, and Jessie's daughter Rachel turned toward me with a considering look.

"Could be that this was the only way God could stop her running," she said, and her sister, Sara, nodded.

"And maybe that jail she's in will be the mirror she finally can't turn away from," Sara said, and I remember looking up, startled, when she said it, recalling months back feeling that God had been the mirror to my own fears . . .

"Percy told Shawn they think she poisoned the man she was married to before him—and Percy thinks she might have done it, too," Willa said hesitantly, like she was trying to decide how much to say. Finally she set her sewing in her lap with a sigh. "He said he had caught her about a year back sprinkling something over his food, and it hadn't set right with him. He said he started making his own meals after that, and that's when she got meaner."

"It's no wonder he was always acting like he was scared to death of her," Lillie said softly, her big, round eyes reminding me of Mercy's.

We all fell silent then, lost in the shock of what Willa had told us, trying to imagine what could ever cause a person to go so bad. Jessie was the one who finally broke the silence, sensing the thoughts on everyone's minds. "Don't matter how she got that way. What matters is the Lord has stopped her now," she said firmly. "And maybe because of that, Percy and them girls will have a chance."

"It's like what Preacher said, Mama," Sara said then. "Sometimes it takes things like this for people to understand who God is—and who *they* are to him."

Everyone nodded and picked up their sewing again, as if Sara's words had settled at least that much in our troubled minds. Soon enough, our talk turned to the building of the church, and a hopeful light came into Willa's eyes at the mention of it. It was the first time I could recall that she had asked for something so humbly as she did when she asked us then to pray for mild weather so Preacher could have the cut lumber delivered.

On the way home, as I thought of the hope Willa had for a new life with Preacher, I also thought of Percy Audrey and the life he was leaving behind. My mind turned back over the years of our knowing him as the kind, gentle soul that he was, but how we never had the chance to know much more than that. Then the idea struck me that, as bad as it looked, maybe this was a new wind blowing into Percy's life now, too. Maybe, I thought, we all might just get a chance to see the man God intended for him to be all along . . .

The mustard seed is the *least* of all seeds, Preacher had

said, and I guess if people were to look at any one of us, that might be what they'd see, too: the least of all. But I remember what the Word says happens to that tiny seed: "When it is sown, it groweth up, and becometh greater than all herbs." It becomes a *tree*, Preacher said.

Quinn told me tonight he's had to put two more weak heifers in the calf corral to be fed, making it four now. "But I think our hay just might last until the snow goes off," he said with a note of relief. "Funny thing is, I thought this would be our worst winter for losses." He shook his head in wonder. "But so far it has turned out to be our best winter. Who would have ever thought?"

"Well, *God* would have," I said simply, and he looked at me for a long moment, then we started smiling at each other at the same moment.

February 4, 1874 . . .

Clear, cold day today . . . but calm, too. There's a stillness in the air that has everyone—including me—looking up to the sky from time to time as we work. It's like we all feel something is brewing.

I just pray it isn't more snow.

February 5, 1874 . . .

No snow has come—but we were surprised by both Willa and Peach showing up at the ranch today. I think we're even more surprised what's come out of the visit, though.

I'd heard the wagons and went to glance out the window to see who had come when I spotted Gale unhitching their teams for them. Then I saw them both turn and shuffle through the snow together toward our cabin, and I fairly ran to the kitchen to make sure I had some coffee and johnnycake to offer them. When I finally opened the door, they were both grinning.

"It looks like we both had the same idea," Willa said. "I was just telling Peach here that fine minds think alike."

"Well, I don't know 'bout that," Peach said, ducking his head, embarrassed, but it wasn't hard to see he was pleased, too. "I was just thinkin' mebbe we both had a hankerin' for comp'ny, is all."

Willa looked at Peach for a moment as we sat down at the table, then she said he was probably right about that, with Preacher still being gone and all. That's how the whole conversation about the church got started.

"Well, I bet he gits tired o' bein' away, too, Miss Willa," Peach said kindly, already reaching for his second piece of cake.

"Well, he doesn't complain," Willa said with a small smile. "But then, we're at the mercy of this weather, and how can you fight that?" She sighed. "It's like trying to wrestle the wind."

"Well, I don't know 'bout that, neither," Peach said, narrowing his eyes as he glanced at her sideways. Willa's philosophical side always made him uneasy. "But my grand-pappy used t' say when there's a will there's a way, and he was 'bout the smartest feller I knew of. They don't give jes anyone *gradgiation* papers from the third grade, you know."

"Well, he sounds smart to me, Peach," I said, and Peach fairly beamed at me.

"He sounds smart to me, too," Willa said, grinning. "As far as *will*, we have that. It's just trying to figure out a *way* now . . ." Willa's voice trailed off, and no sooner than it did, Quinn and the children came tromping in for the noon meal. Pretty soon Jack and Lillie were there, too, after spotting Willa and Peach's rigs. Then Medicine Weasel and One Shot and Jessie and her family came, too—"To see what the ruckus was about."

By the time we had the meal prepared, the cabin was nearly bursting at the seams: children playing, men talking by the fire, Jasper on the lookout for anyone who hadn't taken his hat off while Honey lay curled up in the corner with her pups. It would be hard for anyone to imagine a clear thought coming out of the pandemonium at that moment—harder still to imagine the answer to the raising of our church coming from a confirmed "heathern" such as Peach—but it did.

In no time at all we had agreed on his plan to pitch in and start building—weather permitting or not. And I don't think any of us could be more excited about it. Except for maybe Willa, that is.

"Lunatics," she declared, sniffing to try to keep back the tears as she rocked Mara Lee. "But what would I ever do without you all?"

"Nodunt!" Mara Lee declared then, looking up at Willa with a grin, and we all laughed. Especially Willa.

"I guess that settles it then," she said wryly.

Quinn just told me that Gale has gone on to help Peach get started clearing the spot for the church and that he,

Patrick, Jack, and John-Charles would meet them first thing in the morning to start felling the logs.

"What about me, Pa?" Rose said, looking crestfallen, and I heard Quinn go on to tell her that it was men's work and he was sure that once everything got started, there would be plenty of work for us to do, too. I saw right off that his explanation didn't set well with Rose, and I admit, it didn't set well with me, either.

"Oh, we're going, too, Quinn McGregor," I said, setting my pen down. "I didn't practically *walk* from Missouri to California, survive deaths, desert, and a mudslide for you to tell me I'm too *delicate* to help." Rose looked at me in awe then fairly beamed, and I saw Quinn grin, too, as he glanced over to Patrick.

"I guess she told me, didn't she, son?" he said, and Patrick nodded somberly as he fed more wood into the fire.

"You can't look them in the eyes, Pa," he said sympathetically. "I learnt that from Rose. If I don't let her see my eyes, then she can't guess how to get at me." He shook his head as he stood up and dusted his hands on his trousers. Then he added gravely, "If you don't learn that quick, you're done for."

We all laughed then—even Patrick—but only after he took a quick glance my way and smiled his best charming little smile at me . . .

Quinn came up and hugged me from behind as I was writing this, saying he should have known better than to expect me to stay home. Then he whispered into my ear, "Our little lad has a lot to learn still, as well," he said. "Because I knew I was *done for* the first time I laid eyes on you, lass. And I've never regretted it."

"I haven't, either," I said, pretending to busy myself

with writing again. "Not much, that is," I added and managed to keep a straight face until I glanced over my shoulder at Quinn, and we both started to laugh.

February 6, 1874 ...

"When God answers our prayers, he sure does it up right, doesn't he?" Jack said, grinning as we all packed for town this morning, and all of us couldn't agree more. We had all said we'd pray for good weather before bed last night, but the beauty before us was more than we could've hoped for: a warm, mild wind had came from out of the blue, blanketing the valley with a calm we hadn't felt in months as we watched the sun shoot through the gaps of the mountains, lighting up the sky with pinks and golds. Even Medicine Weasel and One Shot seemed to perk up as they trotted by on their horses to keep watch on the cattle while we were gone.

By the time we reached town, we were all in good spirits—especially Jack, who soon spotted Peach and Gale as we pulled our teams in just past the mercantile. It appeared Peach was having a time of it, getting his mules to listen. He was so engrossed in arguing with them that he didn't hear us clamber in behind him.

"Why, Peach, what are you doing in the middle of the road with a wagon full of brush?" Jack yelled, grinning, and we saw Peach startle, then he and Gale both looked over their shoulders at us.

"Well, I'm fixin' to git this church spot of your'n cleared if'n ya don't give me a heart failure first," Peach said grimly, and we all laughed, hopping down from the wagons to lend him a hand. Not long after we got Peach's wagon back on its way to dump the brush, I turned to see Percy watching us through the window of the mercantile.

Percy waved at us. Then, as if he'd made a sudden decision, he turned and disappeared from the window. The next thing I knew, he was crossing the street to meet us, Zora and Nora fairly running behind him to keep up.

"Peach told me what you all plan to do," he said, looking at each of us one by one. Then he cleared his throat. "The minute he said it, I got it in my mind that I need to donate any nails or tools or whatever other supplies you might need from the mercantile to get our church going. I suppose Preacher has made more of a difference in my life than he'll ever know, so me doing this is a small thing, compared to that."

"Mother is going to be livid if she finds out," Zora said suddenly as she came up from behind him, her pale brows creasing in a worried little frown. Percy turned to his daughter with a frown of his own.

"I think I know what I can donate and what I can't, Zora Audrey," Percy said in a firm voice that none of us had ever heard before. "I ran this mercantile fine before your mother, and I will run it again."

I don't know exactly how to describe it, but when he said those words, I felt as if something had suddenly changed . . . as if Percy's life had taken a sudden new turn. I saw his girl Nora step forward then as if she sensed it, too, looking at her pa with a kind of newfound appreciation.

"Do you want me to help you load those things up, Father?" she said, and when he smiled and nodded yes, I saw Zora go over to help her sister, looking back over her shoulder at her pa with a thoughtful look.

"You're a good man, Percy Audrey," I said, turning

back to him. "I just wish Leah would have seen that sooner."

"Oh, I haven't given up on her yet, Mrs. McGregor. I pray for her every day, just like I pray for me and my girls," he said. Then he crooked his finger for me to come closer, dropping his voice to a whisper. "I even mailed her one of them new Bibles we have in the mercantile . . . I guess it's up to her now, if she decides to read it."

There was such a hopeful look on his face after all that he had been through that I wanted more than anything for it to stay.

"That's the best reason I can think of for us to keep praying for her, don't you think?" I said, and Percy smiled a grateful smile at me.

"Yes ma'am, Mrs. McGregor," he said. Then Peach was there, arms folded across his skinny chest like a small general as he looked between the two of us.

"What are you two jawin' about while there's work to be done?" he asked with a spark of mischief in his eyes. I saw everyone turn back to look then as Lillie, Jessie, and her girls all exchanged amused looks.

"We were talking about praying," I said, crossing my own arms, and Peach couldn't help himself from grinning.

"You know, you and that family of your'n is about the prayin'est bunch I ever did see," he said, shaking his head. Then he peeked up at the sky. "But it seems to be workin', and I ain't one to mess with success." He walked off, and the children scampered behind him, all talking a mile a minute, Mercy bringing up the rear, struggling to keep up as she pushed Mara Lee in her carriage.

"Percy, I just have one thing to say to you, now that

we've endured a dressing down from Peach together," I said as we watched them go.

"What's that, Mrs. McGregor?" he said, glancing over at me with a sudden bit of anxiety on his face.

"Stop calling me Mrs. McGregor," I said in my best somber tone, and I saw Percy start to smile again. I smiled, too. Then we headed together up the small hill where Preacher's "tent of many colors" stood and joined hands with everyone to pray before we set to helping clear the spot nearby where our new church would stand.

Willa arrived not long after we had finished the clearing and was quick to pitch right in as we began setting down the stone foundation. Then suddenly Mrs. Pumphrey and Widow Spence were there, too, working right alongside of us, and as dirty and hard as the work was, none of us seemed to notice; we laughed and talked and sweated—and sometimes even groaned—while the men shook their heads, grinning as they stripped and notched the logs. But we placed that foundation together, stone by stone . . . and I couldn't help thinking as I looked around at all the tired, dirty faces—the faces of all of our children, of Jessie's children and grandchildren, too—that we had laid more than just the foundation for our church. Rose said it best when she scrambled into the back of the wagon at the end of the day with Patrick and Gale, her new honey-red hair peeking out beneath the handkerchief under her bonnet, her face streaked with dirt and grime.

"It's just like we're one big family now," she said happily, and I saw Gale look over at her and smile.

I am so tired tonight—we all are—but I couldn't help putting this to paper. We will be back to town again come morning for another day of work. But today . . . Today was the beginning, and I don't ever want to forget it.

February 7, 1874 . . .

Dawn is peeking up over the mountains, and we will be leaving soon. There is a chill in the air that wasn't there yesterday, but it hasn't dampened anyone's spirits, judging from the talk and laughter going on just outside as the men get the wagons ready. And now Mara Lee is up.

I pray you prosper us in our work this day, Lord, and that you lead us in all that we do . . .

We have just come home, and I guess the only way I can describe this day is to say it went from good to bad to good again . . .

We had just half of the shell of the church stacked, pleased that the logs were fitting so snug in place while the children ran about with shiny new buckets from the mercantile, gathering up sticks and woodchips that would fill the gaps before the chinking, when a freak storm blew in out of nowhere. First cold rain, then sleet, then finally snow, all in a matter of minutes as we tried to pack our wagons. Then Percy was yelling in the midst of it all for us to take cover in the mercantile, and so we did, dripping wet and shivering as we filed into the store. It was no time at all before Percy got the stove going full strength, and we all helped each other peel the layers of clothes from the children first then tended to ourselves in a kind of disappointed silence.

"I had been hoping Shawn would see it finished when he got back," Willa said finally, breaking the silence with what we had all been thinking ourselves as we sipped the hot cider Percy made for us.

I saw the children gather at the large window of the mercantile then, staring out into the storm, and I saw Patrick look over at Willa before he glanced down at Jessie's grandbaby Noel, who was holding his sister Clary's hand tight as he stared wide-eyed out the window.

"That sure is a beautiful church," Patrick said softly. "I like the way that chinking stands so white in the sun against the dark logs, the way the windows look so clean and sparkly . . . and look at that steeple with the cross on the top. I think Preacher's gonna love it, too."

"Can you see it?" he said, kneeling down next to Noel, who looked again and then nodded happily. I saw Gale and John-Charles move in closer to stand next to them then as they gazed out the window, too.

"I see it, Patrick. I think I've always seen it that way," Gale said, and they smiled at each other. John-Charles glanced from them back to the shell of the church and stared for a long moment. He was known for his honesty, so I knew he wouldn't say anything unless he was sure. Finally a look of relief crossed his face, and he nodded. "I see it," he said.

"I see it, too," Mercy said, bobbing her little head, her short blonde curls sticking out every which way from under her handkerchief. Then Rose, not to be left out, blurted out in her impulsive way, "Oh, I see it, too." But I saw her turn back when she thought no one was watching, squinting her eyes *just to be sure*, and we all smiled at each other. All except Willa, who was looking out the window with such a wistful look that I couldn't help thinking Patrick had helped her see the vision, too.

"Here it is," Quinn said then, causing us to turn, and I saw him sitting on a little stool, his large frame hunched over one of the new Bibles Percy had told me about. "I was just sitting here and for some reason, that story of Nehemiah came to mind." Quinn looked up at all of us for a moment. "I kept thinking how a lowly slave had such a heart to rebuild Jerusalem's gates that God gave him favor . . . so much that the king himself even gave him letters to get the timber he needed. And how he started to build in spite of everyone's doubts." Quinn smiled, wry-like. "And I remembered what happened next, how everyone and everything started coming against him. But most of all, I remembered what he said when that happened." Quinn ducked his head to read again: "'The God of heaven, he will prosper us; therefore we his servants *will arise and build.*'"

Jessie and her children looked at each other with small smiles, nodding to themselves.

Then Patrick said, "What happened next, Pa?" and all the children (adults, too) moved closer to where Quinn sat. "Listen to this," he said, and he started reading again.

"'So built we the wall; and all the wall was joined together unto the *half thereof*: for the people had a mind to work.'" Quinn looked up at the shocked faces of the adults and the puzzled faces of the kids and smiled again.

"What's that mean, Pa?" Patrick asked.

"It means they had the wall halfway built," Quinn said patiently, "about like our church is right now."

"And then what happened?" Patrick asked, knowing something good was coming.

"Then they were attacked again," Quinn said, "just as the gaps in the wall were beginning to be closed. But Nehemiah knew what to do . . . he prayed."

Then Quinn looked over at Patrick. "Because of his faith in God, I imagine Nehemiah could see the wall finished before it really was—just like you're seein' our church."

Patrick smiled a shy smile, then we all joined hands— even Peach, who looked slightly dazed as Widow Spence took his hand in hers. Quinn began the prayer, and we each added to it as we felt led, even the little ones, and before long, we felt a new strength fill us . . . a kind of peace that told us we were going to finish our church.

I saw Jack and Lillie smiling at each other, and even Willa, who seemed so discouraged, perked up considerably after that, walking down the aisles and looking at goods as the storm raged around us outside.

"Why, Percy Audrey, you've been doing quite a bit of changing, from the looks of these cheap prices," Willa said at one point, dropping a tag from the bolt of goods she had been casually looking at. I saw, too, that Percy had been strengthened then, the way he didn't shy away from her words.

"Sometimes change is a good thing, Willa Cain. You of all people should know that," Percy said, drawing himself up to his full height. We all looked at Willa, whose brows were arched high like she couldn't quite believe what she'd heard.

"Well, it's about time," she said, then added, "You beat all, Percy." And when she started to laugh, we did, too. But it was the look on Peach's face I'll never forget, so thoughtful, as he glanced shyly Widow Spence's way before he turned to leave . . .

The storm blew over not long after that, and we all took our leave, waving to Percy and the girls, to Mrs. Pumphrey, and to Widow Spence as we headed out of town. It was a cold ride home, but the children were snug under the straw and blankets. And truthfully, I can't really remember much of the cold myself as I sat next to Quinn. But I do remember us talking nearly the whole way home about all that had happened and how faithful God was to put the story of Nehemiah on Quinn's heart to read.

"Do you know what's funny, Callie?" Quinn said. "From the time I started reading that scripture, I felt it lifting my spirits the same as the others."

"That's how God works," I told him, snuggling in closer to him as we finally made our way down the snaking road that led into our valley. And as I watched the light of the moon glancing off the snow-covered hillsides, I realized that something had changed in me, too. I realized it didn't matter anymore about the snow or the scorched earth beneath it. What mattered was I felt good coming home again.

I told Quinn that, and he wrapped an arm around me, hawing the team on toward the ranch, and even by the pale light of the moon I could see the quiet joy on his face. "That's how God works," he said finally.

February 8, 1874 . . .

Sabbath. The sky is dark gray, choked with snow clouds hanging down so low that you might think if you reached your hand up, you could touch them. But we are all determined not to concentrate on the clouds or the thought of more snow. Instead we try to keep our minds focused on the scripture Jack read to us from the Bible this morning, and such a beautiful scripture it is:

> Let thy work appear unto thy servants, and thy glory unto their children.
> And let the beauty of the LORD our God be upon us: and establish thou the work of our hands upon us; yea, the work of our hands establish thou.
> — Psalm 90:16–17

I'll never forget how Jack had looked up after reading that, how his eyes met Quinn's and they both smiled at each other—or the look on Jonah's face, his eyes closed and such a sweet smile coming to his lips as he listened to the words.

Or Mercy as she tugged on Jack's shirt saying, "It said *children*, Pa. That means us, doesn't it?" . . . how the rest of the children beamed when he said yes, that meant them . . .

Thank you, Lord, for this day, for reminding us again that you are in charge over all that is yours. I *know* this church is yours . . . and I know we are, too.

February 9, 1874 . . .

Another day working on the church. Mother Nature's threat of snow came through just as we rolled into town, but so did our prayers. Peach said he'd never seen a more determined group than us, the way we all ignored the cold and snow and set to finishing the top part of the shell. "Even yer little ones," he said, shaking his head as he watched the kids work like anything to fill the gaps in between the logs with their buckets of sticks and wood shavings.

"We're in the Bible, too, Peach," Mercy announced with grave importance. "It says 'their children,' and that's who we are. You can even ask my Pa."

"Oh, I reckon I see the truth of it in your eyes, Mercy," Peach said, gently touching a weathered old hand to her head. When he looked up I saw his eyes catch with Widow Spence's, and I saw, too, the thoughtful smile on her face as they did . . .

We took our noon break not long after that; a picnic of sorts in the mercantile, with hot biscuits from Mrs. Pumphrey and venison stew Peach had made outside in a covered iron pot over a fire, adding to it the bacon we'd brought. Then Percy broke out some canned fruit, and we poured that over the johnnycakes Jessie had brought for a fine dessert. We had such a good time, praying and talking together, that it didn't even seem to matter about the snow as we all tromped back out in it together to work again. I don't know how to explain it, but the snow and cold we had to deal with seemed to only draw us closer together . . .

I saw it in the way Quinn walked back up that hill with Gale after the noon meal, and heard it in their laugh and talk. Then I heard Quinn ask Gale about his parents, and I saw the boy duck his head for a moment, looking off across the town before he spoke.

"They left awhile back, Mr. McGregor," Gale said finally, and I heard Quinn ask him what he meant by "left."

"I went to check on them when the scarlet fever came, and they had already gone," Gale said. "Cleaned about everything out of the cabin, too."

There was only a brief silence, then I heard Quinn say, "Well, I guess you're ours for good now."

Gale smiled over at him then, the biggest smile I'd ever seen. And it was then that I recalled Rose's words: "It's just like we're one big family now," she'd said, and I thought then that truer words had never been spoken as I watched Quinn put his hand against Gale's back, just like a father might do a son.

I witnessed so much of that spirit all day long: the way Jessie, Rachel, and Sara worked side by side with me, Willa, and Lillie as we mixed the chinking in the mercantile so it wouldn't freeze and took turns tending Mara Lee then running outside with our buckets to shove it into the gaps before it could freeze . . . and how Jack and Widow Spence both lunged for John-Charles at the same time when he was nearly struck by one of the logs . . . and Percy, swallowing his fear of heights to help Quinn and the boys with the shingles . . . even Jonah helping Mrs. Pumphrey up when she slipped in the snow, telling her she was as light as a feather when she tried to shy away, saying she was too heavy for him to lift.

It comes to me as I'm writing this that the good Lord isn't just helping us build a church, but a real family of people who truly care for each other . . .

But most of all, of people who care for him.

It appears we weren't the only ones determined to see our church finished.

Jessie just left after waking us up by banging on our door so hard she nearly scared us all to death. She had Medicine

Weasel with her, and the poor old fellow looked a sight. Seems that sometime after midnight he realized one of the sick heifers we were keeping in the barn had escaped, and he took it on himself to go fetch her. One Shot had found him an hour or so later, nearly froze solid, and by the time they brought him to us, he wasn't much better. His face looked mottled, and his ear was so red and swollen it stuck out at a frightening angle, cracked right at the seam where it joined his head. I set to dropping some warm glycerin in it with a turkey feather, but he kept pushing me away.

I finally asked him what was the matter, and he said, "Promise me you won't tell Jack Wade about this." I asked him why, and he looked at me with those rheumy old eyes of his and said, "Just promise me."

He finally let me and Jessie doctor him after I promised not to tell, although I can only pray we did some sort of good, as bad as that ear looked. Jessie and I stood on the porch after that to make sure he and One Shot got safely down to their lodge, and that's when she turned to me suddenly with a funny look to her face as if a thought had struck her.

"You know what I think, Callie?" she said, smiling softly. "I think Medicine Weasel didn't want Jack to know because he knew Jack would stay here at the ranch to make sure he was all right." She turned to peer back down at the lodge. "I think that old Indian wants to see that church finished as much as we do."

February 10, 1874 . . .

It has been a long, bitter-cold day but worth every moment we've spent putting the finishing touches on the outside of the church. The chinking has been laid in, and oilcloth covers the windows for now until we can get the glass shipped in. Quinn, Jack, and Jonah are down in the barn with the boys finishing up on the steeple we'll bring to town with us tomorrow—made, by the way, just as Patrick described it that day . . .

Lillie, Jessie, and her girls are here, sewing for all they're worth so we can get the wagon sheets put together for a floor covering. We're all feeling the race against time now as Willa has told us she thinks Preacher will be home by the thirteenth.

I am bone tired. Rose is calling, "Come on, Mama!" as she sews on her part of the cover, and Mara Lee hollers from her crib, "Here, Mama!" and everyone laughs.

I suppose I could pray for patience, but the thing is, it's always been the one prayer of mine that gets answered *so quick*.

February 12, 1874 . . .

I have missed a day of writing in all the rush, but we have gotten so much done, little journal, I think you will forgive me. I can spare only a moment now, as we are fixing to leave again.

Yesterday was spent cleaning and scrubbing the inside of the church so we could lay down the new floor. And now that it is down, we are ready for the furnishings.

Quinn, Jack, and Jonah have just finished the benches, and our boys—will wonders never cease—have made Preacher a new pulpit out of white pine, sanded so smooth it feels like silk.

For the front of the pulpit Gale has carved a beautiful cross that would make the angels sing. And the smile he just gave me for saying so could as well . . .

Later—

I think we are all going to see a very surprised Preacher, come tomorrow—if we don't all drop from exhaustion before we *can* see him.

And before I do drop for the night, I want to say thank you, Lord. Thank you for the blessings of bringing this unlikely group of people together and making us a family, for guiding us through all the tough times and for giving us a preacher who has such a heart for you, a preacher who has taught us that you *can* see those tiny mustard seeds within us and that, more than anything, you want to watch them grow . . .

February 13, 1874 . . .

I don't think any of us have ever witnessed Preacher go speechless, but we did today . . .

We were all hiding inside the church, watching as he pulled up with Willa in the wagon. He looked to have been saying something when he glanced up, and that's when we saw Preacher go completely still as he looked in shock from his tent to the little log church that stood next to it and then to the steeple above. He quickly climbed down from the wagon, and in a few long strides, he had opened the door to see us all standing inside. His handsome face looked tired from the days of traveling but dazed, too, as if he couldn't believe what he was seeing.

Then, without a word to us, he stepped inside, and we parted to let him pass, watching with grins on our faces as he stepped forward and gazed in wonder around the freshscrubbed room, his eyes traveling from the floor to his old stove we'd shined up and built a crackling fire inside. Then he moved on to the new benches and the pulpit that stood at the head of the room. He walked over to it and ran his hands over the cross Gale had carved, lingering over the tiny vine of thorns that wrapped around the cross and the single rose that lay at its foot. Then he turned to us and smiled a shaky kind of smile.

"It's like you said, Shawn," Willa said with her own shaky smile as her eyes filled with tears. "It's easier to get the hook in than it is to take it out. We just didn't want to do without you anymore . . . "

Preacher looked at Willa, then his eyes went to each and every one of our faces. He seemed about to say something, but it was as if he couldn't form the words.

Then that six-foot-tall Preacher, built like a lumberjack, sat down hard on one of the benches in his new church . . . and he cried.

I will say this: A man crying makes other men more uncomfortable than I've ever seen. Jack and Quinn suddenly found their feet very interesting, and Jonah looked over at Jessie as if trying to find something other than Preacher to fix his eyes on. Percy tried to be sympathetic as he had broke down before, too, but even he didn't know where to look. Peach just looked ill. It was Medicine Weasel who surprised us all by slowly shuffling over to Preacher in a pair of ancient boots he refused to toss even though they pinched his toes horribly. (Boots, by the way, that Jack swears the old Indian took off him all those years ago when he found Jack lost and half-dead in the Montana wilderness.) Medicine Weasel touched Preacher's shoulder gently, and when Preacher looked up at the old medicine man, his face suddenly lit up.

"Why, Medicine Weasel, I thought you said you would never set foot in a church," Preacher said, smiling.

"That is because this is not a church," Medicine Weasel said simply with a soft smile coming to his old face. "It is a home—*Grandfather's* home—and I like to visit the homes of those that mean much to me."

"That's exactly how I felt when I walked in here," Preacher said, looking up at Medicine Weasel in wonder. "That this was his *home*."

We all started to smile again then, glancing at each other with tears in our eyes, for it did look like a home. All that time we had secretly worried about our little log church not being like the "real" churches in other towns, the kind we imagined Preacher would prefer—built smooth with hewn lumber and painted white. All that worry had been for nothing. The smile on Preacher's face was proof of that. But more than that was the truly peaceful feeling that we were in God's home . . . that he was right there with us, too.

Preacher came around and hugged each of us then, and when he got to the children, their happy grins and laughter, mixed with ours, made me feel as if we were having more of a family reunion than a church opening.

What a reunion it was, Lord. I don't ever want to forget this day, the way my loved ones laughed in it or the feeling that you were there, surrounding us with your love as Preacher said grace over the meal we had all prepared. I don't ever want to forget the looks on our little ones' faces as they realized they had been a part of something greater than they could have imagined.

"For the Lord thy God blesseth thee," your Word says.

And I believe you did.

Quinn and I have been watching Patrick as he sleeps tonight . . . wondering if he thinks we have forgotten his birthday is tomorrow with all the rush to finish the church. It doesn't surprise me that he hasn't said anything. He is so much like his father at times . . . such a good, honorable little spirit dwells inside that stocky little body that it amazes me at times that he is mine . . . that God has given me such a gift.

I wonder what this new year will bring him. Whatever it is, Lord, I pray your face continues to shine upon him and that you bless him as much as he has blessed me.

Bless all of us, for that matter.

Because that would be a better gift than anything I could ever think of . . .

February 14, 1874 . . .

It's so hard to imagine Patrick being nine today—but then, I admit, sometimes I forget he is *only* nine, too. For example, there's what he said this morning when we all woke him up, singing "Happy Birthday" and filling his lap with the little gifts we had made for him once he got settled on the settee.

"I had so much fun yesterday, I thought that was kind of my birthday, too," he said, looking at all of us with a shy kind of grin. But as he opened his first gift, a new hunting knife from Quinn, we saw the little-boy light come to his eyes as he grinned and lifted it up to show Gale and John-Charles.

"Just wait till we go fishing, come spring," he said. Then he went on to open the rest: a buckskin jacket from Jack, a horse blanket from Jessie, and an elk-tooth necklace from Medicine Weasel. Gale made him a beautiful carving of a trout, and Rose had fashioned him one of her horse-hair whips she's so good at braiding.

But Rose, being Rose, could not bear to let her brother's birthday go by without some form of teasing. She waited until she felt the time was just right. It just happened to be when he pulled the new trousers I'd made him out of the brown wrapper. He had been begging me to "fox" him some trousers like Quinn and Jack wear. They're really just britches with a heart-shaped piece of buckskin sewn into the seat and down the inside seam of the legs to save wear from riding. But it was clear Patrick was tickled to death over them.

"What kind of pants are those?" Rose said suddenly with a mischievous look to her eyes, and Patrick frowned, sizing her up before he went on to speak.

"The same kind of pants Pa and Uncle Jack wear," he said warily.

"Well, you're gonna look strange wearing them," Rose announced cheerfully.

"I like 'em," Patrick said, frowning again.

"Well, you're *gonna* look strange," Rose repeated, then she smiled, and the cat was out of the bag. Patrick grinned, too.

"Well, I *like* them," he said again, refusing to let her have the last word. So, just to throw him off *and* because it was his birthday, Rose let him.

"I'm sure glad *we* don't act like that," John-Charles said, looking down at Mercy.

"Me, too," she said, but we saw her unconsciously cover her bear's mouth as she slid a glance toward Peach. We all couldn't help but laugh.

We have been so blessed the past couple of days . . . but I am so very tired, too. Now that the little ones are bathed and asleep, it's all I can do to write this.

I *have* to get some sleep. Sabbath is tomorrow—in our new little church—and I am looking forward to it more than I can say.

February 15, 1874 . . .

Sabbath, and what a moving message it was that Preacher spoke to us today. I have never felt such a gladness in my heart as I did today, listening to his words. I don't think any of us will forget them . . .

"A beautiful day, wouldn't you say?" Preacher said, smiling broadly as he stood behind his new pulpit. We all smiled, too, nodding amongst ourselves as we looked around in wonder at how many people had braved the bitter cold to be there. "With this warm fire in our stove and so many friends and family here, I can't imagine it being a better day to share a story," Preacher said, and suddenly all the rustling and shifting in the seats stopped as everyone leaned forward to listen.

"It's the story about another son who was given his father's inheritance," Preacher said. Then he held up his hand. "Remember, I said *another* son—I think we all know the story of the prodigal son well enough. No, this is a very different story, one I hope you will remember for a very long time."

Preacher looked around, his eyes falling on Peach for a moment, then he went on.

"Shortly after this son is given his inheritance, he is sent on a long journey to a faraway land. He's been told by his father not to let on to too many people about his wealth because there are some who would try to steal it from him . . . and though this son was the sharing type, his father also told him there would be some people who didn't deserve for him to share it with them. This son knew how wise his father was, so he listened. 'You'll know the ones who are our kind of people and the ones who aren't,' the father assured him. 'In particular, watch out for the men that go around acting holy, waving to everyone they see on the street, but behind closed doors steal widows' lands for their own.'"

"I knowed some rough characters like that once," Peach blurted out suddenly, unable to contain himself, and everyone chuckled, including Preacher. Then he went on: "Now, I have to say, even knowing this, the journey for this young man wasn't an easy one. It seemed every time he was doing something good, someone had it in for him."

A few of us caught Peach nodding vigorously and looking like he was itching to say something, but then

Widow Spence put a hand on his shoulder. Peach turned to her and smiled, shy, then seemed to calm down after that.

"But a funny thing happened," Preacher went on, a glint to his eyes as though he'd seen Peach. "The more trouble that came his way, the more he saw that money wasn't the answer. See, this son decided he would use the part of his inheritance he best knew how to handle—the riches he'd never really had to deal with because his father had always handled that when he lived at home. Instead, he remembered the *words* his father had taught him . . . words of wisdom that had been sown so deep in him that no one could ever uproot them . . . "

Preacher paused for a moment then and looked around at us.

"If he came across people who were being greedy, he would try to persuade them of a better way, saying, 'It is better to give than to receive.' If he found people judging others, he tried to warn them so they wouldn't have to face a hurtful end: 'Judge not, that ye be not judged.' And when people brought their children to him so that he might just touch them, only to have his disciples try to send them away, he held his hand up and looked upon the little ones with love, saying, 'Suffer the little children to come unto me, and forbid them not: for of such is the kingdom of God.'

"You see, my friends, that Son, *Jesus*, knew that the childlike faith our children have, the complete love and trust, is what Jesus had for his Father. He knew that the greatest part of his inheritance God had given him to use on this earth was love.

"He knew that his wealth was his love.

"God has given us our homes and land as part of our

inheritance, but the other part of our inheritance—the most important part—is our love for others. I can't imagine a finer showing of love than that shown by the folks who worked so hard to build this church—or better, 'God's home,' as a very wise man so aptly named it."

We all looked over at Medicine Weasel, who had suddenly straightened his back and had what might pass as a pleased smile on his face.

Preacher stepped away from his pulpit then and walked closer to us. "Can't you feel it?" he said, looking around at us with such a beautiful look on his face. And suddenly I did feel something settle over us in the room. Preacher smiled. "God has granted us our inheritance; he has given us our land. And he has also given us his Word." Preacher held up his Bible for all to see. "*This* is how we learn to tend our land. *This* is how our seeds of faith will grow . . . how they will stay sown so deep that no one or nothing will ever uproot them.

"These words are what will remain when everything else passes away, for the greatest of all of these is love. That's what he has given us here. And that is what he asks us to give as well, to share our inheritance with others just as his Son shared it with us."

We all fell silent, feeling the truth of Preacher's words come over us like a balm to our hearts. Then, instead of Preacher walking to the door of the church like he usually did, he sat down next to Willa, and we were surprised to see Percy walk slowly to stand in front of the pulpit.

"That was some fine words you spoke, Preacher," Percy said, his voice a bit shaky, and Preacher smiled at him and nodded. Percy turned back to us then, and that's when I noticed that he was holding a paper in his hands.

"I asked Preacher if I could read this after the sermon,

and I have to say now, it seems more fitting than ever. This paper I'm holding is a letter from Leah—and it was written as much to all of you as it was to me." Percy looked at all of us and took a deep breath, then he began to read.

First Leah asked about the girls, then she told Percy she was thankful for the Bible he had sent her. She went on to say that she realized she had to get caught to be found again. She said she had been living a lie for so long that she had forgot who she was before she started the lie.

Then Percy read in a shaky voice that she had been really reading the Bible in earnest—that she really wanted to know who God was and not just hear of him from others . . .

What he read next surprised us all.

She told him to ask two things of us. The first was if we could forgive her . . . and the second was if we could mention her in our prayers.

No one seemed to be able to say anything for the longest time. Then I felt Quinn stand up next to me. "Preacher, I was thinking this might be a good time to pray for her, with everyone here now, don't you think?"

Preacher said he did and asked us all to stand and join hands, and as we did, Percy's eyes met mine, and I saw an endurance and a kind of peace that I had never seen before. And that's when I realized what that feeling was I had felt earlier.

It was a new wind from God, coming into Percy's life . . .

February 17, 1874 . . .

The sound of water is everywhere, running off the rooftops and trees; rain is falling down through purple skies, running here and there like warm fingers tugging back the shroud of snow to bring to life again what's beneath it. It came in with the Chinook that roared up the valley from the south last night. The cattle felt it first, and thinking it gave them the go-ahead to roam, they're now spread out everywhere, huddled wet in pockets throughout the valley, their legs bogged down in old snow and new mud.

The men have been out in it since before dawn, moving like molasses through the sludge-covered hills and coulees. I am so grateful for Gale and Jonah to be here to help—Peach, too. He showed up out of the blue this morning, saying he just "happened to be passing by." He really is such a dear friend to us . . . Quinn thinks God's hand is what nudged him our way nearly five years ago.

"Think of it," he told me last night. "Who else *but* God could convince a 'confirmed heathern' to push us into getting our church built?" We grinned at each other and shook our heads; I don't think either of us will ever get over the wonder of seeing God's handiwork in our lives— or the lives of others . . .

I best close for now; they will be in for the noon meal soon, and already I can picture their muddy footwork on my clean floor . . . I think Rose can see them as well; she looks from the window with a grim look to the floor then back to Mara Lee, who has just pulled herself up to stand next to my chair. Mara Lee claps then looks startled as she wobbles, grabbing ahold of the chair again. Steady again, she looks over at Rose with a grin.

"You just wait, Bird," Rose declares gravely. "It might be all fun, now. But the older you get, the harder the work gets."

It is taking everything in me not to laugh . . .

Muddy footprints notwithstanding, the men have succeeded in getting our cattle back down closer to the lower valley. I don't think I've seen a more tired or happy crew than them as they finally called it quits for the night, sliding their chairs back from the dinner table, sharing looks of kinship and gratitude. Seeing them like that, I couldn't help thinking how God's hand has nudged all of us together in a way that I never would have imagined.

But it's what Peach said to me just before he left that I don't think I'll forget.

I had a pretty good idea he was wanting to say something, the way he kept glancing over at me through dinner, and it didn't take long to find out I was right. He lingered around until everyone had filed back out to the barn to take a look at one of the calves, then he announced almost offhandedly that he thought he'd go—but didn't budge.

I asked him if he would like to walk out on the porch with me then, and he looked almost grateful for the suggestion.

"It don't matter how long I live out here. It's always a shock when warm weather shows back up," Peach said, looking up to the sky. Then his voice got quiet. "But there's a lot of things that kin shock a person . . . " Peach glanced at me sideways for a long moment then went on, as if a decision in his head had been made. "Like I surely never thought I'd set foot in a church," he said. Then he cocked his head to one side. "The strange of it is that even when we was gettin' it built, I didn't think of doin' sech a thing. It was jes like I was walkin' through them doors a'fore I even knowed what I was doing. But ya know what,

Miss Callie? I'm glad I did. I ain't ever been one for flowery sayin's, but the way your Preacher spoke of thet Jesus got me thinkin'. Because Jesus sounded like the kind of feller I wished I had knowed . . . "

"He's not gone, Peach," I said, feeling my eyes well up with tears in spite of my trying not to. Peach saw the tears, but for the first time didn't seem uneasy about my show of emotion. I saw his face soften as he nodded, then he looked back over the dark valley.

"Widow Spence said much the same. Gave me one of them Bibles from the mercantile, too, and tolt me to read it fer myself," he said. Then his voice dropped almost to a whisper as he looked up at the sky again. "An' from what I've read so far, I reckon if'n anyone had the right to beat ol' death, Jesus sure did." Peach turned back to me as if a thought had suddenly occurred to him.

"Does it tell in the Good Book how he beat it?" Peach asked. And when I grinned and told him yes, it did, his head bobbed up and down, and I saw an almost childlike excitement come over him.

"I was hopin' it did," he said, smiling.

He left not long after that, and as I watched him ride away I couldn't help remembering how amazed his face had looked, trying to figure out just how he had walked through those church doors without really thinking on it first.

But you know what, little journal? I'm not so amazed.

February 20, 1874 . . .

It seems that early spring, like everyone else that has blown into our lives in a day, has decided to stay for a while. I have been so busy trying to keep up with the endless rounds of meals and mud that I haven't had much of a chance to write, but Peach has been awful strong on my mind since we talked. I found a scripture in John this morning after praying for him, and I think it's fitting:

And the sheep hear his voice: and he calleth his own sheep by name, and leadeth them out. And when he putteth forth his own sheep, he goeth before them, and the sheep follow him: for they know his voice.
—1 John 10:3–4

There is another scripture I remember reading, about how God knows us before we are even in our mother's womb, and I can't help thinking *that* is why we know the sound of his voice so well when he calls . . .

I wish I would have thought of it to tell Peach when he was here! I'll have to remember it when he comes again . . .

Well, good-bye for now, little journal. Mara Lee is hollering to be let down from her crib. Quinn caught her trying to shimmy out of it herself last night and laughed, saying she'll be walking in no time, as determined as she is to catch up with the others.

Seeing her grinning little face looking over at me as I write this, I don't doubt it.

February 21, 1874 . . .

I can hear the last of the huge cakes of ice sliding off the roofs of the cabin, the bunkhouse, and the barns, hitting the ground with such thuds that Jasper and Honey run to bark at the intruder. I've never thought of spring coming as an intruder, though—more of a friend, I think. The kind of friend that makes you want to do *something* . . . Already everyone is thinking ahead to those somethings, talking of fishing and swimming, of planting gardens . . . of getting married—the latter being the talk of the evening—well, *that* and Rose.

Willa has finally set the date for April and has asked us all to help make her dress, and of course we agreed, which led to us discussing it after dinner . . .

"I'd make ten weddin' dresses to finally get that girl up the aisle," Jessie sniffed as we all sat at the table, talking, and everyone smiled.

"Well, if Peach has his way, you might just be asked to make another dress," Lillie said then, and Jessie nodded sagely.

"There's another one that needs to quit dawdlin' 'fore it's too late."

"Is there anyone around here that you *don't* have to keep after, Mama?" Rachel said, laughing as she looked over at Sara.

Jessie grinned. "Not that I kin think of offhand," she said, and we chuckled.

"She's always kept after me, ever since I was born," Rose said suddenly, and we all looked at each other in stunned silence as none of us had even seen her in the room. Then Jessie lifted up the tablecloth, and by the wide smile on her face, we knew she had found Rose.

"Now, what you doin' under there easedroppin' on folks, Rose McGregor?" she asked, trying to sound firm.

There was a brief silence again, then: "Oh, I don't know anything about *ease*dropping, Jessie, but I do know this is the best place to sit and listen for news to put in my journal."

"Ever think I might have a good reason to keep after you, little sis?" Jessie asked, and we just couldn't hold our laughter in any longer.

Rose scrambled out not long after that, her short honey-red hair curling up every which way as she sat down next to me with a charming little grin on her face. "So, is Peach really gonna marry Widow Spence?" she asked, all eyes.

As I hugged her to my side, I couldn't help wondering what I would ever do when that funny, impulsive child who had breezed into my life one day . . . what I would ever do when she decided to breeze out of it.

I can only pray that Willa and Preacher are as blessed with such a family as Quinn and I have been given. And dear old Peach—I pray that he and Widow Spence do somehow find their way to each other . . . I don't think God ever intended for any of us to be alone; otherwise it wouldn't hurt so much when we are . . .

Makes me think of something Jack said in a letter to me so many years ago, but I have never forgotten it, for how it made me laugh—and made me think, too. He said, "As fickle a bunch as we humans can be at times, we can't seem to live without each other either, can we?"

If he asked me that today I would tell him no, we can't live without each other. And then I would tell him that if any of us could learn one thing from Preacher and never forget it, it would be that our wealth *is* our love.

March 3, 1874 . . .

We witnessed the most beautiful thing tonight. It was after dinner, and we were standing on the porch, reveling in the nice weather and talking, when I heard Gale say, "Look up there." And we looked up to where he was pointing and saw a huge swash of what looked to be blue-white fire arcing through the night sky, as if God himself had took his finger and decided to suddenly move some stars. Then, just as we were watching, a lone star appeared to separate itself, and it came shooting across the sky, lighting up the valley below for a moment.

I heard everyone let out the breath they had been holding in then, and as Quinn put his arms around my waist I looked over to where the children were standing in front of Medicine Weasel's lodge and saw their awe-filled little faces. Then I saw Jessie, Jonah, and his sisters holding hands and Jack and Lillie smiling up into the night sky. But it was Peach's face I don't think I'll ever forget as he stood next to Gale, so filled with wonder. Then he turned to look at all of us, his smile saying he was glad to be sharing the moment with someone.

"It's kindly like he was puttin' on a show jes fer us, weren't it?" he said with such childlike earnestness, none of us had to ask who *he* was . . .

March 6, 1874 . . .

All day today as I have done the wash outside, scrubbing the clothes and hanging them on the line, I have seen tiny bits of green life poking up, trying to push free from the mud, and for some reason those words of Preacher's keep running through my mind about the tiny mustard seed in us, struggling to break free from the earth so it can reach up to touch his light . . .

The Other Side of Jordan

Peach surprised me this morning by showing up at the door and asking if I would like to take a ride out through the valley with him, and I'm so glad I did.

We rode in silence most of the way until we got to the high meadows, then as if something about where we were suddenly made his decision for him, Peach dismounted and came over to help me down off my horse.

"Looks like spring is really here now, Peach," I said, smiling as we looked out over the valley together. He nodded, a pleased look coming to his old face.

"Yes, and it looks like that new grass has taken root, too," he said, sweeping his hands through the air in such a poignant but grand gesture I felt as if he were introducing me to the greatest performance I would ever see . . . and in a way, that's just what he did.

I turned and looked across the valley to where he had pointed and saw the new grass that had begun to take over the scorched places of earth. There was still some curvy patches of bare earth here and there, almost like little trails, but as I looked at those little trails, I couldn't help thinking of what Jessie had said about the mending scars being new roads for us to follow. And for some reason, I just knew that the grass would grow stronger than before along those scars of earth . .

"Most folks kindly like to think an old feller like me wouldn't like change—but I think I would, now," Peach said, cocking his head sideways to look at me thoughtfully. "Havin' hope agin, it helps you look forward to something new, don't it, Miss Callie?"

"Yes, it does," I said, and he nodded.

"Well, you helped give me that hope, and that's why I wanted to bring you out here, to give you some hope, too," he said, and I had the oddest feeling come over me when our eyes met. It felt like everything else had faded away—Peach's old, shabby clothes that had seen better times, the scruffy mane of hair he could never seem to tame. So many differences stood between us, yet they were suddenly gone, and all I could feel was Peach's spirit and mine, recognizing each other, like long-lost family members feeling each other's love. It was like we were suddenly brother and sister.

I hugged Peach then, startling him at first, but then I felt his old, weathered hand rest on my shoulder, felt him pat my back in a way that I hadn't felt since my pa died.

For some reason, the memory of a story I'd read came to my mind then, the story of a man who said he'd had a sparrow land on his shoulder for a moment while he was hoeing his garden . . . and how that moment had made him feel more important than if someone had clipped a priceless jewel to his shirt. Right then I felt I knew what that man had meant as I stood there hugging Peach while a warm spring wind whipped around us.

Only my jewel wasn't a sparrow but a grizzled old man everyone called Peach—who was better than any jewel I could ever imagine.

So, this is what you planned for us to be, Lord, my heart whispered as we finally rode back down to the valley together. *This is how we would've all been if we hadn't believed that first lie . . .*

I can't help thinking even as I write this now what a tragedy it is that the devil took that kind of love from us— but what a sheer blessing it is that Jesus brought it back . . .

Because that love, after all, is as much our inheritance as this land.

PART FOUR

Bountiful Harvest

Then Joshua divided the INHERITANCE among the people and God Shined His Face on them and the people were glad because God has a nice Face. And he gave them a lot of good stuff, too.

By Rose McGregor
Almost 14

March 13, 1874 . . .

If I could imagine such a thing as paradise, I would imagine it a bit like our valley in the spring—only better, I'm sure . . . But still, there is something about the sharp, clear blue skies and the hills rolling with new green and the immense mountains that rise up with such grandeur in the distance that makes you almost believe it's never been touched by the world. That somehow God cupped his hand over it and let what we call progress walk on by, unseeing . . .

Quinn and I were standing out on the porch, drinking coffee together this morning, when I told him how I felt, told him that it made me realize just how blessed we are to be trusted with such a gift.

"Did you ever think that's why he gave us this land, Callie?" Quinn said. "That he knew our love for him allowed us to see that it *is* a gift?" He took Mara Lee from my arms and kissed her cheek, and when she laughed at him, he looked over at me and smiled. It was then that I noticed how deep the lines at the corners of his pale blue eyes had become—little trails of weather and worry, Mama used to call them . . . But it was in those lines that I saw so much of our lives, too. Saw the young man he'd been when we first met, so alone in the world . . . but so willing to love and never giving up on me in spite of my fears. Then I saw the husband that bore our hardships as well as others' with such compassion. But most of all, I saw the man that God had made him into along the way.

"Nothing compares to what he gives us, does it?" Quinn said softly, his voice filled with such emotion that all I could do at first was nod.

Then I looked across the land again, to the hills starting to dot with the white faces of cows and calves trotting down to dip their muzzles in the river, and as strange as it sounds, as I watched them, I felt like I, too, was drinking in that crisp, clean water—like the newness of it was running through my blood, and I looked over at Quinn and smiled.

"Do you remember what I asked you that time we danced in the middle of that prairie we found along the trail?" I said, and he hesitated for only a moment then smiled, too. The memories of our journey west on that wagon train were still as strong in him as they were in me.

"You said, 'Where have you been all my life?'" he said, and when I asked him if he remembered what he had answered, he said easily, "Looking for you." I saw a softness come to his face as he said it, and in my heart I felt the effect just the same as the first time he said it.

"I'm glad you found me, Quinn," I said, blinking back my tears. He pulled me to him and kissed me, Mara Lee laughing delightedly between us.

The door of the cabin flew open then, with Rose peeking out first. "They're doing it again," she announced gravely, and we saw Gale, then Patrick, add their faces to the opening in the doorway. Gale looked at both of us then grinned happily. "You kind of get used to it," Patrick said, shaking his head as he grinned. "They've been doing that as long as I can remember, and I don't think they're going to stop."

Quinn and I started laughing, and this time, I didn't think of it as the poetry of the moment dying. I couldn't help thinking it only became more beautiful with the laughter of all our children surrounding us, joining in with ours.

Quinn was right: *Nothing* compares to the gifts God gives us.

Well, our muddy little troupe cleaned up nicely after helping drive the cattle today—and after my promising to read another Bible story. Such an eager look to their little faces as they gathered around my rocking chair in the crowded cabin this evening . . . Medicine Weasel and One Shot looking almost comical, their heads rising high above the others as they, too, sat cross-legged on the floor, waiting for the story to begin. But it was how the gathering ended that made it such a night . . .

"John the Baptizer," as Patrick calls it, was the story they finally agreed on, and I noticed when I got to the part where John said, "I indeed baptize you with water, . . . but he that cometh after me is mightier than I . . . : he shall baptize you with the Holy Ghost, and with fire," that a sudden spark came to Medicine Weasel's eyes. He glanced over to One Shot, who nodded and said something in Blackfoot, and they both leaned forward. I started up again, reading how Jesus, in order to teach the people humility, came to the Jordan to be baptized by John . . . how when he was standing in the water, praying, the heavens opened up and a dove came and rested on his head and how the people heard a voice saying, "This is my beloved Son, in whom I am well pleased." And as soon as those words were out of my mouth, Medicine Weasel and One Shot turned to Jack, talking excitedly in Blackfoot, and we all stopped to listen.

Jack said something back. Then he turned to me and smiled, but it was John-Charles who spoke up first as he leaned forward from in-between Patrick and Gale.

"They want to be baptized, Aunt Callie!" he said, glancing back at Medicine Weasel. His grandfather nodded at him to go on. "They said they had been feeling like God was waiting for them to do something more before he could bring the Holy Ghost for a visit."

None of us said anything for a moment, and in the silence I couldn't help thinking how easily the two Indians had accepted the gospel . . . with such childlike acceptance that I couldn't help wishing everyone looked at God and his Word that way.

"One Shot, too?" I asked when I finally found my voice, and John-Charles nodded then smiled, seeing the surprise on my face.

"Oh, One Shot's been listening all along, too. He and Grandfather pray together all the time now," John-Charles said easily. "He just doesn't like to speak our language. He said God hears him just as good in Blackfoot."

"Well, now, I bet he does, too," Jessie said then, looking over at her children then back to me, her dark, old face filled with a kind of soft understanding. I saw Gale glance around to us all with a thoughtful look to his face. Then the rest of the children looked back up at me, ready for me to keep reading as if what had happened was the most natural thing in the world . . .

"You can go on reading, Mama," Rose announced, the pleased smile on her face echoing everyone else's in the room.

But no one looked more pleased than Medicine Weasel

and One Shot as I opened that Book again and began to read . . .

As I write this tonight, I can't shake the feeling that the Lord is once again at work with his plan in our lives . . . in my mind's eye I can imagine a great hand gently patting the earth over the seeds that it has sown. I can imagine the water, much like what I felt running over me today, falling upon that earth so clear and pure . . . and I can imagine the most beautiful, expectant smile waiting for those seeds to sprout up and grow. What was it that Solomon wrote? Something to the effect of the generous soul will be made rich, and "he that watereth shall be watered also himself."

March 15, 1874 . . .

Our Sabbath morning woke us up to a warm, sunny dawn—warmer than usual this time of year—making our trip to town so pleasurable after all the chill and snow that we almost didn't make it to church on time. But we weren't the only ones; Preacher came rushing in a little after us with Willa on his heels, looking flushed but pretty as she took a seat next to us, grinning sheepishly while Preacher explained he and Willa had taken a walk through the garden this morning before church.

"Ah, the things we do when we are in love," he said with a teasing look in his eyes. Willa blushed hard then, and when we all burst out laughing, Preacher did, too. But after a moment, his smile softened.

"But you know what?" he said, looking around the room. "When I was out there gardening, it came to me what I needed to say to everyone today. It happened just as I had raised up from planting a new row, and when I looked out across the yard, for some reason I was struck by the way the trees in some areas looked almost like they were grouped together like families. And that got me started thinking about how that came to be. How once a tree grows to maturity, it begins to drop seeds of its own . . . How those seeds will be planted right into the earth . . . and begin to take root during that first winter of their lives. And when they are ready, they will spring up and grow tall and healthy to stand next to that tree . . . " Preacher paused then and looked around at us, as if a thought had just occurred to him.

"But what if that tree didn't drop its seeds?" he asked. All of us kind of glanced to each other with puzzled looks on our faces. Preacher just nodded and opened his Bible as if he expected as much.

"Well, it talks about that very thing in the Gospel of Matthew," he said. "Does anyone remember the story Jesus told of the man who went on a journey and left his servants to handle his wealth for him?

"Well," Preacher went on, "the first servant took the portion he was trusted with, and he doubled his master's wealth. The second servant did the same. But the third servant, thinking he was wise, buried his master's wealth so that no one else could touch it. Now, when their master returned and found what the first two had done, he was pleased as anything. 'Well done, thou good and faithful servant,' he told them. 'Thou hast been faithful over a few things, I will make thee ruler over many things: enter thou into the joy of thy lord.'"

Preacher looked about the room then, his face turning serious.

"But that last servant? The one who buried his master's wealth? Scripture says the master cast the unprofitable servant into the 'outer darkness.'"

Preacher held his hand up and stepped away from the pulpit so he could stand in front of us. I caught sight of Peach sitting next to Widow Spence with Medicine Weasel and One Shot on the other side of him. The three men leaned forward together just then. Behind them, Widow Spence's eyes met mine, and we smiled.

"I can tell you right now that God, our Father, does not want that to happen to any of us," Preacher said, and we saw the three relax a bit. "But, you see, he had a Son who so loved the world that he invested *all* his inheritance in us . . . including *his own life*. So, how much is he really asking of us to share what we have of him?" Preacher shook his head sadly.

"Not much, I think . . ."

"I don't think it's too much to ask, either, Preacher," Peach said suddenly, unable to contain himself any longer. Then he looked toward Medicine Weasel and One Shot, who nodded their agreement, and we all smiled—Preacher included.

"That's a good thing, that you can see it that way, Peach," Preacher said. "Because I can tell you what he hopes to see happen for each of us. Jesus said it best, so I will read you his words . . . " Preacher ducked his head and began to read: "'When the Son of man shall come in his glory, and all the holy angels with him, then shall he sit upon the throne of his glory.'" Preacher closed his eyes for a moment, and the soft look on his face made me think he was imagining that very thing. Then he opened his eyes and looked at all of us and smiled, reciting the last words by heart: "'Then shall the King say unto them on his right hand, Come, ye blessed of my Father, inherit the kingdom prepared for you from the foundation of the world: for I was hungered, and ye gave me meat: I was thirsty, and ye gave me drink: I was a stranger and ye took me in: naked, and ye clothed me: I was sick, and ye visited me: I was in prison, and ye came unto me. . . .'"

Preacher glanced over at Percy and smiled, and I saw the tears in Percy's eyes as he smiled back. Then Preacher turned and looked at the rest of us.

"Jesus has given us a portion of his wealth, our inheritance as children of God . . . But what I want you to ask yourself is, What are you planning to do with yours?

"I know what I want to do," Preacher said, his voice going soft as he sat down on a chair next to his pulpit, looking down at his hands. "I want to love like Jesus loves. I want to see every seed around me take root and grow tall to stand beside me . . . I want to be the hand someone reaches for in the dark of their lives. And I want to know the Lord will send such a hand to me in the dark of my life, too . . .

"I want people to know how close God really is—Jesus is—and I want them to feel his love like I do." Preacher smiled a small smile and gave a little shrug as he looked to us again.

"But that's just me . . . "

"No, Preacher. 'Tis all of our hope," Quinn said then, the passion in his voice matching the Preacher's. I saw the whole room glance our way, and I knew some of the new folks were sizing up Quinn in much the same way they did

Preacher, thinking it couldn't be weakness that led such a strong ox of a man to speak like he did. Jack turned to Quinn then, and the two smiled at each other like they were blood kin.

"Amen, brother," Jack said, and I felt a catch in my throat. When I glanced over at Lillie and the rest of our family, we all echoed an amen to his . . .

It wasn't until after everyone else had filed out that we learned why Peach, Medicine Weasel, and One Shot had been in such a state; they had decided amongst themselves before the service that they ought to be baptized *today*. And as soon as Gale heard of their plan, he decided he wanted to be baptized, too. So, with our eager Preacher in tow, we all headed for a stretch of river near the picnic grounds, laughing and talking as the children scrambled in all directions. Percy offered to carry Mara Lee for me while we walked, which gave me the chance to ask him how he was faring.

"Well, Leah hasn't sent the Bible back, so I'm looking on that as good news," he said with a look of good-hearted endurance. I saw that his girls looked better as well; their faces had filled out some, and their hair was neatly braided, though Willa was right about their needing a woman's touch with the way their dress hems hung lopsided from Percy's attempt at sewing. Those hems were noticed by every woman in the group as we exchanged looks of silent understanding before we turned to watch the baptisms begin.

Despite the warmer than usual sunshine, the air was still brisk, and the water was icy cold. So the baptizing was a slightly rushed affair. Peach was first to go into the water with Preacher, then Gale, followed by Medicine Weasel and One Shot. Preacher quickly baptized each one in the name of the Father, the Son, and the Holy Spirit. And I don't think there was a dry eye to be found along that river as we watched their beaming, steamy faces come out of the water. It was all over in about a minute, and when Preacher finished with One Shot, Jessie turned to me and smiled.

"Looks like you have quite a little forest growing around you now, honey," she said, and when I realized what she meant, I smiled back.

"Not just me, Jessie," I told her. "That little forest was planted by all of us." We turned and looked at everyone lined along the banks, adults and children, and I couldn't help thinking how we did look like a grouping of trees, both old and young. I saw Mrs. Pumphrey say something to Willa and heard her and Lillie laugh as the newly baptized Christians—the old trapper, the solemn Indians, and young Gale—quickly hopped out of the water and shakily reached for the blankets and buffalo robes we all rushed to wrap them in. Then I saw Widow Spence hand Peach her picnic cloth to wipe his face, and that's when I realized that none of them had a dry change of clothes.

It was Percy, bless his sweet soul, who got the idea to bring the "boys" back to the mercantile and gift them all with new trousers and shirts. So we all headed for the store, teasing our "baptizees" as they trotted behind Percy to the back of the store, dripping and grinning with happiness.

"Now you will be 'putting on the new man' in more ways than one," Preacher chuckled, and we did, too, as the men slowly emerged from the mercantile one by one wearing their new outfits. Peach chanced a shy smile Widow Spence's way, and Gale looked like it was all beyond what he could have imagined. But Medicine Weasel and One Shot both appeared to be in some sort of pain.

"Does Grandfather's Word say anything about having to wear such clothes if we are to remain baptized?" Medicine Weasel asked me with a concerned look to his old face.

"Oh, no," I told him, trying to keep a straight face. Then I couldn't help but smile and add, "As soon as your things are dried out, you'd better get 'em on. Otherwise he might not recognize you!" Medicine Weasel's eyes widened one quick second then crinkled into a smile as he nodded, relieved. One Shot did, too.

"I was hoping you would answer this way. Because these clothes are scratching me to pieces," One Shot announced suddenly *in English*—the only English he had ever spoke. It startled us all so much it was a long moment of shocked silence before we all began to laugh.

Even the children laughed—although I'm not sure they realized what it was they were laughing about. Except for John-Charles.

I'll never forget his wry grin, so much like Jack's, as he shook his head at One Shot . . . or the way he glanced toward his grandfather after that with such a look of love . . . or how his eyes met Jack's and they both smiled wide smiles, as if at the exact same moment they had both found what they were looking for . . .

The only word I can think of to describe it is *home*.

March 16, 1874 . . .

Back to work again today, and what a long day of it. But the weather has held, along with everyone's spirits.

Especially for Peach, who decided to stay over and help us get our cattle to the high meadows where the grass is already growing tall from the warm spell.

"If you folks don't have the Almighty's ear turned to ya, I don't know who does," Peach said as we finally reined in at the mouth of the meadows, watching the cattle trot forward with purpose as they spotted the lush grasses.

Even Jessie, who had been clinging to her mount for dear life only moments before, was captured by the abundant beauty of it all, and I saw her nod then, a satisfied look to her old face as she glanced around.

"He ain't never early, ain't never late . . . " she began.

"He is always on time," we all said together with her. Then we laughed as Jasper and Honey bounded through the grass like rabbits past us as their puppies tried their best to keep up.

We had almost finished with lunch when I happened to spot "Callie," the cow Jack so kindly named, as she headed back down the slopes in the opposite direction of the other cattle. I told Quinn I would go turn her around. Peach looked up from eating, and I saw him frown.

"You best let one o' the fellers do that," he said casually, and Quinn and Jack looked over at him and grinned just as I felt my hands go to my hips.

"Is there any reason why you think I can't handle it, Peach?" I said, and as everyone started to chuckle, I saw a dawning come to Peach's face, then a mischievous grin. He turned to Quinn.

"Guess you might at least try t' convince her t' listen to good advice now and then, young feller," he said to Quinn. "As fer as I've seen, them stringy little ones live a long time."

"Stringy!" I started in, but Quinn was laughing too hard for me to go on. Instead, I turned and marched over to my horse, determined to show Peach just what I *could* do.

And as it turned out, "Callie" had the same thing in mind herself. She trotted resolutely down the hillside as if she meant to show me what *she* could do. And for a while I wondered if she might win. She took me up one side of the slope and down the other and twice around a clump of thorny brush before I think she just got tired of the chase and let me drive her back to the herd.

It didn't take me long to figure out that it had been quite a show, judging by the grins on everyone's face when I finally got back to where they stood.

"Well, I did what I set out to do, didn't I?" I said.

Peach looked over at Quinn. "She don't give in easy, does she?" he said, trying to keep a straight face.

Quinn followed suit, shaking his head sadly. "I guess I'm in for the long haul, Peach," he said with a sigh.

"Well, yes, I kin see that. But it's a mystery to me why you look so *happy* 'bout it," Peach said, shaking his old head, and everyone couldn't help but laugh. Then they laughed harder as Peach tried to help me down from my mount.

"Gimme that little hand of your'n, an' I'll help ya down," he said, and the peace offering of his hand must've put a look on my face, for he and everyone else continued to laugh.

"Aw now, Miss Callie, I was jes joshin' ya about bein' stringy. Why, you have a goodly 'mount of meat on ya." He looked at me hard, narrowing his eyes. "I kin see it if'n I squint my eyes jes right," he added with a twinkle in his eyes. I tried my best fierce look on him as I slapped his out-stretched hand away, but Patrick ruined my act.

"Don't worry, Peach," he announced cheerfully—and loudly enough for all to hear. "Mama's smiling under that old bonnet. I just saw her teeth."

A quiet night for writing tonight, Lord, as everyone has fallen into an exhausted sleep. Everyone except me that is, writing again . . . I remember reading in one of the books Willa loaned me, I think it was Byron, that if he didn't write to empty his mind he would go mad. I don't see my writing that way, I guess. I see it more like a song I write of my life, of all our lives—a song that sings through the trials as well as the triumphs . . .

March 18, 1874 . . .

Mara Lee took her first steps on her own today, and Jack was convinced it was in honor of his birthday.

"Look, she's coming right for me, sis," he said, grinning, as Mara Lee crossed the room on wobbly legs, a determined look on her little face. But instead of Jack, she went for the table, reaching and stretching her chubby arms toward the half-eaten birthday cake.

"Mine!" she declared, and Jack laughed, picking her up. Then Jack, being Jack, leaned her forward and let her plunk her hands right into the cake, laughing again as she quickly stuffed them into her mouth.

The rest of us groaned, but Jack just sat back with his little niece, a pleased look on his face as she offered him some, too. When his eyes met mine, I saw so much of Pa in

him . . . so much of the easygoing kind of love we had
grown up around that I couldn't help but smile.

Jack smiled, too, the corners of his green eyes turning
down like little half-moons like they always did when he
was touched by something. Medicine Weasel said something in Blackfoot then, and Jack nodded and said
something back before turning to me.

"He was trying to figure out our word for beauty
because he wanted to say we have a lot of beauty in our
family."

"Well, what *is* our word for beauty, then?" I asked, and
Jack smiled.

"Closest I could ever figure what the Blackfoot meant
by beauty was *love*. But they don't have a word for love.
Medicine Weasel told me a long time ago, they didn't
need the *word* to love."

"Beauty almost sounds better, doesn't it?" Lillie said,
smiling softly, and everyone couldn't help but agree—
especially Mara Lee, who picked that moment to put her
sticky hands on each side of Jack's face and kiss him on the
cheek, making all the children laugh.

Patrick turned to Gale with a shrug. "See? Bird's
already doin' like Mama," he said. "I think it's kind of in
the girl's blood."

"You boys just wait. One day it's going to be in your
blood, too," Jack said, grinning, and they all groaned. All
but Gale, who just looked happy to be included in another
family tradition.

My tears have went and blurred some of this page, but I can't seem to help myself . . . Jack just came by the cabin to give me a poem that he'd written on the trail right after our sister Rose had died. He said he found it in Mama's old Bible and thought I might like to have it. Then he shuffled his feet a little, looking at the floor as he handed it to me.

"Remember when I was alone with John-Charles in that cabin after his mother, Raven, died? That's when I found it in Mama's Bible. I was glad I did, too; it always reminded me of you whenever I read it," he said, softly. "But now that we're here together, I thought you might like to have it . . . "

Here's what it says:

CALLIE, REMEMBER WHEN?

Remember when
The sunrises captured our youth, and marigolds
   along with your smile played joyfully
   in the sun?

Remember when
We swam in dirty water with broken grass clippings
   in our hair?

Remember when
We walked and joked and laughed about our
 lives to come
   with Rose by our side?

Remember when
You were saving up for that dress, but bought
   me a new pair of boots instead?

Remember when
We thought heartache could never
    touch us?

Remember when?

I showed the poem to Quinn tonight after Jack left and said, "Can you believe Jack wrote this?"
He just smiled and hugged me to him. "I can believe that Jack loves his sister more than anyone could imagine," he said. "Except for me, that is. I could imagine it."

March 19, 1874 . . .

From the porch I watched Jack breaking in a green horse this morning just as the sun was rising up over the mountains, and I wish I could put to paper the beauty of what I saw . . . Maybe *beauty* isn't the right word. Maybe it's *awe*. Or maybe it's just a gratefulness to have witnessed the moment, to have seen the look on Jack's face as the horse sunfished, the dust coming up to meet the golden rays of light hovering above the corral . . . Watching, I couldn't help thinking about all the nights I worried over my wild, reckless brother. Worried that I would never see him again . . . and ached for a world that might never know the true heart that lay underneath all the wildness.
But God knew . . .
He knew all along. I realized that truth this morning as I watched Jack. Because even now, the wildness isn't gone. God has just shown him how to claim it. All the days and nights that we had lived through the fever, through the

trials of this past year, they're gone now, and Jack's way of celebrating was what I saw before my eyes.

As strange as it sounds, the words "a man after God's own heart" kept whispering through my mind as I watched Jack finally rein the horse's head toward the corral gate and nudge it into a dead run across the valley. I saw the joy break over his face as he rode across the land, drinking it in like he was seeing it again for the first time, and I thought of that story in the Bible telling how King David danced through the city to praise God. I knew then that that was what Jack was doing.

Dancing.

When I turned to go back inside, I caught site of Medicine Weasel standing outside his lodge watching Jack, too. I saw him clapping his old weathered hands together as he watched, as if he knew the beat of Jack's dance by heart.

March 23, 1874 . . .

Medicine Weasel surprised me tonight by pulling a pair of tiny moccasins out of his buckskin jacket just before he left for his lodge, telling me they were for Mara Lee. "So she won't slip and fall on the grass anymore," he said, adding that "it is a bad thing for one so young to get discouraged trying to walk.

"I can make another pair for her, once the buffalo come," he said, smiling at me with his rheumy old eyes. I must have looked like I had never heard the word *buffalo*, for Medicine Weasel ducked down and put his hands to his head, two fingers up, mimicking the shaggy beasts. Then he looked up at me, crooking his finger for me to bend close.

"You wait and see; they are coming," he whispered. "I know these things."

March 24, 1874 . . .

I have been washing and hanging clothes all day, back and forth, back and forth: Fetch more water, boil another panful, find someplace that isn't already draped with wet clothes, blankets, or linens . . . all the while watching Medicine Weasel and One Shot come out of their lodge to stare off toward the distance like they are waiting for someone.

And now they have me doing it, too.

March 27, 1874 . . .

Medicine Weasel was right. The buffalo *did* come . . . I just wish I could shake the low feeling I've had ever since seeing them. Even Medicine Weasel tried to cheer me up.

"Do not look sad. We've seen a great thing today," Medicine Weasel told me with a smile tonight after dinner. I had the oddest feeling, too, seeing him walk over and hug first John-Charles, then Jack . . .

But as he shuffled his way down to his lodge, his old shoulders stooped over by age, I had to wonder at the weight those shoulders have had to carry . . . thinking of all he has had to endure since we whites have come west . . .

I admit, the feeling that swept over me earlier today wasn't one of "greatness."

When we gazed out over what Jack says will be the last of the great buffalo herds, I couldn't help feeling plain sick, for lack of better words. Over and over in my head tumbled pictures of the monstrous stack of bleached bones I saw last year when we rode through Miles City.

Today when I looked over at Jack, I could almost feel the emotion passing between us—thankful to see the herd but ashamed, too, knowing our own people had been pushing the slaughter. Are still pushing it.

Without really thinking, my eyes fell on John-Charles then, wondering where he would fit in it all. I waved to him to come to me, but he sat, mute, on his pony between Jack and Medicine Weasel, his long hair whipping in the wind, his tawny face turned up to the sky, his mind as far away as the clouds he peered up at. I leaned over and tugged at the reins of Rose's pony and called to Patrick and Gale, then I pointed out over the vast valley of raising and lowering humps of black.

"*This* is Montana," I told them with a tremor in my voice, praying they would understand what they were witnessing . . . and wondering if they would remember this day after the crowds came and buildings rose to meet the sky like cheap imitations of the mountains I'd fallen in love with. This was the Montana we'd all fallen in love with . . .

Suddenly John-Charles was there beside me. He looked at me for a long moment; those green eyes so much like Jack's stared and stared, and I saw the wisdom in them, saw the Solomon to Jack's King David. John-Charles tilted his head to one side with a slow, easy kind of half-grin, and I knew he understood my feelings—but had seen past them, too.

"*We* are Montana, Aunt Callie," he said simply, and I watched him ride off to join Jack, Medicine Weasel, and the other men. Then I heard their laughter as they rode over the slope toward the herd.

And now that I'm writing this, I think I understand that feeling I had when I saw Medicine Weasel with John-Charles and Jack. Medicine Weasel had realized it before I had: His old life has been replaced by a new one now . . . and so has Jack's . . . and John-Charles is the thread that wove them together.

I can't help thinking how beautiful life is, how my brother, who had searched for peace nearly his whole life, had been blessed with a son who would give it . . .

March 30, 1874 . . .

We have all been working on Willa's dress every spare moment we've had over the past few days. Even looking on it as a labor of love didn't help us tonight, as tired as we all were . . .

"My body's went and got old on me without askin' me anything about it," Jessie declared, shifting in her chair with a groan as we sat around the fireplace, sewing. We all chuckled our agreement. But then I saw Rose suddenly look up with a frown.

"You're not old, Jessie," she said in all of her thirteen-year-old wisdom. "You still have lots of time left."

"Don't have much time left in the valley, little sis. Soon enough we be headin' for our new land," she said, glancing over at Sara and Rachel. "And as far as bein' old—you best tell my grandbaby Noel different. He rubbed my face the

other day and says, 'Grandma, did God make you?' Yes, I
say. Then he rubs his own cheek. 'Did God make me, too?'
he says, and I say yes again. And you know what that boy
says, then? He says, 'God's getting better at it, ain't he?'"

We all laughed, but I knew by the look on Rose's face
that she hadn't heard anything past Jessie's saying she was
leaving. I knew it by the pang of sadness that had come to
my heart, and I saw it in Lillie's eyes as well.

Rose didn't utter another word but set down her part of
the sewing and quietly excused herself, shutting the door to
the porch behind her. Later Jessie and I found her still out
there, curled up under several blankets in one of the rockers.

"I ain't helpin' to finish that dress—not if Jessie's going
to leave after the wedding," she said defiantly as we both
knelt down next to her. Then she looked up at us, and we
could see the tears. "'Sides, if Jessie goes, I go, too. And
don't say I can't go 'cause I ain't black. Even Jonah says if
he closes his eyes, I sound just like Sara and Rachel, the
way I carry on, and that's just as good as being black."

I glanced over at Jessie, who, like me, appeared to be
caught between laughing and crying. She shook her head.

"Now, honey, *this* is your home," Jessie said. "But that
don't mean you can't visit me."

"It ain't the same," Rose said, jumping up and running
past Mercy and Gale, who had just stepped outside. I saw a
worried look come to Gale's face.

"She isn't really leaving?" he asked me, and I shook my
head as I put my arm around Jessie's shoulders. After they
went back inside the cabin, Jessie turned to me, and I saw
a bittersweet look to her face.

"Even when the good comes, that don't mean it's

always easy, does it Callie?" she said. I said no, it doesn't mean it's always easy. Then, because neither of us knew what else to say, we hugged each other, standing on the porch in the dark until Lillie came out to join us, too.

"I'm sure gonna miss this valley, miss all of you," Jessie said after a while. Then she took a deep breath. "But I'm ready for me and my family to start our new lives . . . to walk the land the Lord has given us . . ."

We smiled at each other, and that's when I felt a soft wind come across the valley. The looks on Jessie's and Lillie's faces told me they felt it, too. And though none of us said a word, it was as if we knew what that wind meant . . .

March 31, 1874 . . .

Rose is still smarting over Jessie's leaving. The proof of it showed in how cranky she was with poor Gale today. Quinn and I were sitting on the porch after dinner, watching Mara Lee toddle after Jasper and Honey's pups in her new moccasins, when we overheard them on the way down to the river to go fishing.

"Well, maybe you should just go with Jessie when she leaves, then," Gale was saying, the frustration clear on his face even from where we sat.

"Maybe I should," Rose said, picking up her pole and marching off toward their fishing hole.

Gale marched the other way then stopped after a few paces and looked back. I saw him frown, watching Rose continue on, nose in the air—saw him frown harder when he realized she wasn't going to look back.

"Aw, what's the use!" he said, picking up his own pole

again and heading after her. That's when I heard Quinn start laughing.

"I feel the lad's pain," he said, winking at me when I turned to him with my eyebrows raised. "But Rose is young yet. She still has time to work through the legacy of that red hair." He put his arms around me, and I couldn't help but laugh with him. "She reminds me so much of you, you know," Quinn added, and that's when I pulled back to look at him.

"She's not exactly like me, Quinn. *I* would've looked back . . . eventually," I said with a sniff, and we both laughed again.

Still, in spite of our laughter, I can't help thinking of Jessie's words as I write this. *Even when the good comes, that don't mean it's always easy* . . .

We have been so very blessed—more than I could have ever imagined a family to be. But I do feel led to pray for Rose and her ways, Lord. There is something so restless in her that it gives me pause at times. And I worry that, like Jack in his youth, the dreamer in Rose can make the good great and the bad . . . sometimes even better.

"Trust in the Lord with all thine heart; and lean not unto thine own understanding" . . .

And I do trust you, Lord.

April 10, 1874 . . .

It's been another little stretch since I've written in here, but with all the rush and hurry for us to have Willa's wedding dress finished . . . and all the decorating we've done, I just haven't had the time. But it was time well spent;

their wedding today was proof of that. And if ever there was two people who deserved to be happy after all they've been through, it is Preacher and Willa.

Willa looked just like the pictures of those ladies in *Harper's Weekly,* her raven hair swept up in a loose bun with soft strands of curls hanging down, her dress of white embroidered mull fitting her slender figure better than we could have imagined as me, Jessie, Lillie, and the rest of the women beamed at each other with gladness. And Preacher, I don't think I've ever seen him look so hand-some—or so happy—as he stood tall and strong next to Willa while the new missionary who will be taking over for Preacher performed the ceremony.

By the time they said "I do" we were all sniffing back our tears. Mrs. Pumphrey was the first to pull out her handkerchief and wipe the tears that streamed down her wide face, though, and when she caught Mercy looking at her, I saw her wink and straighten her new hat that she wore special for the occasion, saw Mercy smile and straighten her little bonnet in return.

Even Peach wiped away a tear or two then pretended to dust a speck off his new clothes, looking so much shinier than usual that Jack couldn't help but comment on it as we began to trail out to the yard for the party. "Why, Peach, I didn't think you could get any better lookin', but you proved me wrong again," Jack teased, but Peach just glanced sideways at Widow Spence. "That ain't so hard to do. Guess I'll be provin' a lot of folks wrong before long," he said, causing a ripple of chuckles to go through the crowd. But there was a poignancy to the way he looked, too: shy, but determined, like he'd finally caught on to what was important after all these years. I looked around the crowd of us then and saw that we were all catching on, really. But it was Willa who said it best as she hugged all of us.

"Do you ever think God looks down and says, 'Well, now, you're finally getting the hang of what I've been trying to tell you all along?' she said, grinning, and we all couldn't help but laugh. And we laughed again as Mara Lee tried to make a wild dive for the cake on the table, Medicine Weasel catching her up in his arms just in time.

Then we were sniffing again as Quinn surprised even me. I saw him signal to Jack, and together they lifted a huge piece of stone from the back of our own wagon and settled it into the cut in the earth made right by the steps of the church.

"I can't think of a better day to give you this, Preacher and Willa," he said, "to give to *all* of you." We all huddled around then to read the inscription my husband had carved with such care: "Blessed be the LORD, that hath given rest unto his people Israel, according to all that he promised; there hath not failed one word of all his good promise."

"And he *hasn't* failed us," Quinn said, looking to Preacher and Willa. Then he glanced to each of us, his eyes finally resting on Percy, who, we'd heard just before the wedding started, had found out Leah had been sentenced to only five years, for lack of more evidence. Percy cleared his throat and looked to his daughters. "He hasn't failed us," he echoed softly, and then Quinn opened up his Bible and began to read:

"'And Joshua wrote these words in the book of the law of God, and took a great stone, and set it up there under an oak, that was by the sanctuary of the LORD. And Joshua said unto all the people, Behold, this stone shall be a witness unto us; for it hath heard all the words of the LORD which he spake unto us.'"

Preacher looked around at all of us then as he stood with his arm around Willa's waist, and I saw the tears in his eyes, too.

"I don't think I could have imagined a finer group of friends if I had handpicked them from heaven myself," he said. "But I didn't have to, because God did that for me."

And you could tell by the look on everyone's face, we were glad he did, too.

I think the *dilemma* of marriage was fixed on the boys' minds long after we had reached home tonight—especially after them hearing of Peach's proposing to Widow Spence. But it was what they said that got Quinn and me so tickled . . .

"Well, I ain't *ever* gettin' married," Patrick said first as they sat around the fireplace together. Quinn looked over at me and grinned.

"Well, how come them men in the Bible married so many women?" John-Charles asked.

"I don't rightly know," Patrick said slowly. "Maybe they were goin' by the rules—you know, four better, four worse, four rich, four poor . . ." Patrick shook his head then. "I think ol' Solomon had a better idea. Rose said he had a pack of porcupines instead of wives. I think I'd rather have porcupines anytime than some ol' girl."

"I never heard Solomon had porcupines," John-Charles said, frowning.

"Well, all I know is, if he did, he must have been good at handling them," Gale said, adding to the discussion. "Because Rose can be *sharper* than a porcupine sometimes, and I don't think I could handle more than one of her."

"That's right," Rose hollered down from up in the loft where she was supposed to have been reading. "And don't you forget it."

It was then that Quinn and I chose to go out on the porch for a breath of fresh air . . . something that comes in handy when you're having a hard time breathing for laughing so hard.

April 11, 1874 . . .

I've said it before, and I'll say it again: I believe the gifts from God sometimes come in the smallest of packages—and at the most unlikely times. And that is just what happened today as Quinn and I were out at the corral with the horses.

I spotted Rose running toward us and thought she might be hurt by the look on her face, but instead of coming for me, she headed straight for Quinn. And it wasn't until she got closer that I noticed she was cupping something in the palm of her hand.

"He was still in his cocoon when I found him, Pa," she said, her voice shaky as she opened her cupped hands to reveal a tiny, fragile-looking butterfly. "I helped him out, but now he's acting like he's hurt."

"Well, lass, you shouldn't have helped him," Quinn said gently as he knelt down next to her, and I saw Rose look up at her pa with a stricken look.

"But why?" Rose said, near tears.

"Because, lass, the reason God lets the butterfly push and struggle its way out of its cocoon is because while it's struggling, it's also getting stronger. Every time it pushes its little legs, every time it stretches against the cocoon holding it in, it's gaining the strength it will need to fly."

Rose started crying in earnest then, and Quinn smiled and cupped her face with such love that it brought tears to my eyes. "It's just God's way," he said finally, and Rose threw her arms around his neck and hugged him as she cried her sorries into his shirt. "There, there," he whispered. "You didn't know any better, but you do now. It's just God's way."

I stood there for a long time, just watching them and thinking on what Quinn had said. Thinking on it even tonight as I put this to paper . . .

How many times over the years have I questioned in my heart why God hadn't come to our rescue I can't say, but I did. I imagine I've just been too much of a coward to write it until now . . . As if you didn't know already, Lord.

I guess it doesn't seem to matter how old I get, sometimes I still think like such a child, think that you don't know the thoughts of my heart unless I say them out loud . . . unless I write them here. But you knew all along, didn't you, Lord?

You knew, and in your amazing way, you waited for just the right time to give me my answer. Because I'll never forget this day . . . never forget listening to the comforting words of a father explaining to his daughter that having to learn to fight your way through something makes you stronger, that if someone were to step in, you wouldn't earn the strength you need to have for yourself—the strength you were always meant to have . . . the strength it takes to know you *can* stretch your wings and fly . . .

Seems fitting that these will be the last words I'll be able to fit in this journal now. I am a bit curious what the new pages of our lives will bring . . . but hopefully I'm wise enough to know now that there is no figuring it out beforehand. And maybe that's why God tells us to take our lives day by day . . . because he knows us well enough to know that part of the fun on our journey is to look to him and wonder what *is* next . . .

Acknowledgments

The saying "Art imitates life" has come to me again and again as I've thought of my own journey while writing *The Other Side of Jordan*. There have been many moments of intense struggle, as if I were treading water with only my nose above the waves, but there have also been wonderful moments in which I've witnessed God's own hand sweep down upon my life with such beauty and love. I truly believe our wealth is our love—the agape love we give to others as well as the love we receive. So, to all of those who gave me their time, their prayers, and their love, I say thank you for all you have given me. You have made me wealthy beyond measure . . .

To my Lord Jesus Christ: I will always thank you first and foremost for changing my life, for giving me a hope and a future in you . . . and for inspiring me to write for others, to touch this beautiful but troubled world with the message of your love. My deepest desire is to show others how much you truly do care—and how very close you are if they only take the chance to reach out to you.

To my family . . .

My son, Mitch: Thank you for your love, your prayers, for being *you* . . .

My parents, Diana and Joe McClure: For your love, prayers, and all the help and inspiration you have given me.

My brother, Dan Becker, who, by the way, actually wrote *me* the poem I use in the book from Jack to Callie. I love you, bro'!

To my nieces, Raelyn and Kaitlyn Becker; my nephew, Shawn-Michael Becker; and *my grandparents, Doug and Dorothy Vance:* I am so grateful to God for each of you, and I love you all more than you will ever know.

To my friends . . .

Billy Allen, a man after God's own heart. Your awesome songs and music have inspired so many—including me! Thank you so much for your phone calls and prayers and for being such a godly friend. I pray that you and your wife, Rhonda, are blessed and prospered as you continue forward in your ministry.

Kris Bearss, Integrity Publishers: Thank you so much, Kris, for all your prayers, encouragement, and hard work as I was putting the finishing touches to this book. It is a blessing to be a part of such a godly group of people as Integrity.

Shelly Guy: Thank you for being such a great friend, Shell, for all your help and prayers . . . and for making me laugh when I needed it the most.

Chad Gundersen: Thank you for your friendship, your prayers and phone calls, and for all your suggestions that have helped me grow as a writer. They have really meant a lot to me. A special thanks to you and your family for inspiring the names in this volume: Mara Lee (Bird) and Gale; they helped bring those characters to life! I truly pray God prospers and lifts you up in your desire to be a strong voice for Him in the movie industry.

Sue Ann Jones, a great editor and friend. Thank you so much, Sue Ann, for being so willing to take the journey

with Callie and her family again . . . for all of your wonderful words of encouragement, for your hard work,
friendship, and for all your prayers. Working with you
again has been a wonderful experience.

Laurie White: It seems like we have been friends *forever.*
It amazes me we can still come up with new material to
make each other laugh—and always at just the right
times! Thank you, thank you for your true gift of friendship, for your phone calls, and your advice . . . for always
caring. I am so grateful to God for you, Lou.

To my pastors, Jeff and Patsy Perry: Thank you once again
for being such an important part of what has inspired me to
lift Jesus up in the written word. And thank you for believing
in me and for your wisdom, encouragement, and love.

And to all the staff and members of Family Church: Thank
you, thank you for all your help and kindnesses, and most
of all, for your prayers as I was completing this new book.
You all are a true gift from God.